The More Questions Laurie Asked, The Shorter Clint's Answers Became.

"Clint, are you having second thoughts about this?" It was like trying to draw out an uncommunicative stranger.

When he finally looked up at her, she could see the confusion in his eyes.

"I don't think I understand what people mean when they talk about love. They always seem to see it as a good thing. My experience is that it can be a curse as well as a blessing." His voice was angry, warning her to drop the subject. But Laurie couldn't do that.

"I'm willing to go on if you are," she said. It was important to let him know that she cared enough about him to take a chance on their future together. Was she in love with Clint Daniels? As he turned those haunted, blue eyes on her again, she began to think that she was.

"You're either a very brave woman or a crazy one," Clint told her.

Laurie let out her breath. "Maybe a bit of both," she admitted.

Dear Reader,

Welcome to Silhouette Desire! If this is your first Desire novel, I hope it will be the first of many. If you're a regular reader, you already know that you're in for a treat.

Every Silhouette Desire book contains a romance to remember. These stories can be dramatic or humorous...topical or traditional. Each and every one is a love story that is guaranteed to sweep you into a world of passion. The heroines are women with hopes and fears just like yours. And the heroes—watch out! You won't want to read about just one. It will take all six of these strong men to keep you satisfied.

Next month, look for a special treat...six tantalizing heroes you'll want to get to know—and love—in *Men of the World*. These sinfully sexy men are from six different and romantic countries. Each book has the portrait of your hero on the cover, so you won't be able to miss this handsome lineup. Our featured authors are some of the finest: BJ James, Barbara Faith, Jennifer Greene, Lucy Gordon, Kathleen Korbel and Linda Lael Miller. *Men of the World*—don't miss them.

And don't miss September's *Man of the Month* book, *Lone Wolf* by Annette Broadrick. It sizzles!

Happy reading,

Lucia Macro
Senior Editor

CATHRYN CLARE

THE MIDAS TOUCH

SILHOUETTE *Desire*®

Published by Silhouette Books New York

America's Publisher of Contemporary Romance

SILHOUETTE BOOKS
300 East 42nd St., New York, N.Y. 10017

THE MIDAS TOUCH

ISBN: 0-373-05663-X

First Silhouette Books printing September 1991

Printed in the U.S.A.

Books by Cathryn Clare

Silhouette Desire

To the Highest Bidder #399
Blind Justice #508
Lock, Stock and Barrel #550
Five by Ten #591
The Midas Touch #663

CATHRYN CLARE

is a transplanted Canadian who moved south of the border after marrying a far-from-proper Bostonian. She and her husband now live in an old house in central Massachusetts, where she divides her time between writing and renovation. "Three cats and a view of the forest outside my office window help with the writing part," she says.

To my grandmother, Ethel Donaldson

One

It had been three years since Laurie Houston had left her job as a nurse in the emergency room, but apparently the old reflexes still kicked in when they were needed.

And it was a good thing, too, she thought. She was in her office in the middle of a routine follow-up visit with a young asthma patient when she heard her secretary call her from the waiting room.

"Laurie, we need you," he called, and the uncharacteristic panic in his voice had made her get out of her chair fast.

There were several patients in the room, and all of them were on their feet. Over the hushed mutterings of a couple of teenagers, Laurie was aware of a child's frightened voice, asking "Is she dead?" The child's mother was trying to reassure her, while holding onto an infant who turned to look at Laurie with big owl-eyes.

After the first confused moment Laurie realized what was going on. At the center of the scene, a crumpled form of a young girl in a puffy down coat lay in a heap on the waiting-room floor. Nelson, Laurie's secretary, was bending over her. In an instant her years of experience as an emergency-room nurse took over.

"Get her file, Nelson," she commanded crisply, taking his place by the unconscious girl's side. "Who is she, do you know?"

Nelson shot to his feet, obviously relieved that Laurie was in control. "Name's Heather something," he said. "I can't remember what she's here for. Give me two seconds."

Laurie didn't rush him. She trusted Nelson. He was quick and efficient; he'd get her the information faster than she could find it herself at the moment. While he made a beeline for his desk, she turned her attention more closely to the heap on the floor.

The girl looked to be fourteen or fifteen, with fine sandy-blond hair and a delicate frame. Her complexion was probably fair to begin with, Laurie guessed, but now it was utterly drained of color. She tried to recall having seen this patient before, but she couldn't remember the young face.

She didn't like the look of that white skin, and she reached for the girl's wrist to check her pulse. It was rapid, too quick for a simple faint. In spite of her confidence in Nelson, Laurie felt herself growing impatient.

"What happened to her?" she asked over her shoulder.

She could hear Nelson flipping the file folders in the rack on his desk. "She just keeled over," he said. "I thought she looked a little pale, but—here we go." Two long strides brought him back to Laurie's side, folder in hand. "Diagnosed diabetic three months ago. This is her first appointment with you, to talk about diet."

"Not soon enough," Laurie muttered. "Damn!" The girl was probably suffering from an insulin reaction, she thought, but she couldn't be sure without knowing what she had eaten, or how much insulin she'd had. "See if you can get her parents on the phone, Nelson. I'm going to need more information."

"According to the file, her father was scheduled to come with her for the appointment," Nelson said doubtfully. "He's probably on his way."

"Try anyway."

Nelson was already reaching for the phone. "Should I call a doctor, too?" he asked.

"No. Insulin reactions look scary, but they're not complicated to take care of, if you know how." Laurie was on her feet again, heading for her office. She kept a kit there for testing blood sugar, although she rarely had use for it. She made a mental note to compliment Nelson on his housekeeping when she found the kit exactly in its labeled position in her metal cabinet. As she crossed her office to the coffeemaker, grabbing up a couple of small packets of sugar, the patient she'd been talking with moments before asked what had happened.

"Someone fainted in the waiting room," Laurie said. "I think she'll be okay."

She heard the calmness in her own voice, and spared half a second to marvel at it. She didn't *feel* calm; her own heart rate was probably as high as that of the unconscious girl. But thanks to a couple of years of training in the emergency room of the Timmins hospital, she could effortlessly project an image of levelheaded competence.

She headed back to the waiting room, intending to provide the same reassurance to the patients still standing there. Before she could open her lips, though, the outer door opened and a tornado whirled through it.

At least, that was her impression. All the extra adrenaline must have made her imagination especially sensitive, because at first the big man who entered the waiting room didn't seem to be agitated over anything more than being late, from the way he glanced at his watch and hustled himself out of his winter coat. But halfway through the act of hanging it up, he realized what was going on, and then the tornado started in earnest.

He tossed his coat aside and crossed the room in two steps, on legs as long as Nelson's but considerably more powerful. His coat—heavy and expensive navy-blue wool—hadn't quite finished settling into a pile on the floor behind him by the time he was kneeling next to Laurie, and demanding roughly, "What happened to her?"

"That's what I'm trying to figure out," Laurie replied. She was fleetingly aware of a pair of the most brilliant blue eyes she'd ever seen. They were leveled at her in what almost seemed to be an accusation. "Are you her father?" she asked.

"Yes." There wasn't a single resemblance between the girl's finely boned face and her father's strong, almost square features. Heather's sandy-blond hair might someday darken to the color Laurie saw in front of her as the man bent over his daughter again. *The color of old gold.* The thought crossed her mind in a split second, just long enough for her to contrast the burnished warmth of his hair with the icy brilliance of those blue eyes.

And just long enough for her to wonder why the hell she was focusing on the man instead of on his daughter. "I was just about to test her blood sugar," she said, fighting her way back into the calm she'd been feeling a moment ago. "But maybe you can save us some time. When was her last insulin injection?"

"This morning." Briefly, he told her what time his daughter had had her injection, and the dose.

Laurie did some rapid calculating. "Depending upon what she ate for lunch, that dose should have been fine," she said. "I don't want to give her more sugar if this isn't an insulin reaction after all. Doing that could just make things worse."

"Oh, God." The twist of pain in the man's voice made her look up quickly. She couldn't see his face, though; since he was still looking down at his daughter, Laurie couldn't catch a glimpse of those startling blue eyes to let her know what he was thinking. She watched as he took one of Heather's hands, as if he was trying to warm it with both of his own. Laurie found herself unexpectedly fascinated by the size and strength of his hands. They were big and square-boned, like the rest of him, but they were encircling his daughter's fingers with infinite care. He looked like a lion picking up a sparrow it had decided to befriend.

"I'm sure she didn't eat lunch." His voice was ragged with emotion. "Oh, God, honey, I'm so sorry. If I could just figure out some way to tell you—"

The sentence came to an abrupt halt as he seemed suddenly aware that the room was full of people watching and listening, and he raised he head to look at Laurie.

"I'd say it's more than a safe bet that this is an insulin reaction," he said. "I'll explain why I think so later. But right now, I haven't got any sugar with me. Have you?"

Wordlessly Laurie produced the sugar packets she'd grabbed from beside her coffeepot. Raising Heather to a half-sitting position as if she weighed no more than the coat he'd tossed aside, the girl's father held her while Laurie managed to get her to swallow some of the sugar. "Give her a few minutes," she said, as the girl moaned softly.

"Is there somewhere else we could wait?" he asked, looking around the room again. "I don't want her to come to and feel as though she's in a display case somewhere."

"Good point. There's a reclining chair in my office. Let me give you a hand getting her to her feet—"

He brushed aside her offer to help. "I can manage," he said brusquely, and scooped his daughter up in his arms. The girl looked very small against his broad chest, and Laurie couldn't help thinking of how smoothly the muscles in his thighs powered him as he rose to his feet with his burden. Standing up from a kneeling position with a hundred-plus pounds in your arms was no easy trick, but he made it look like nothing at all.

He strode into her office as though it was his own living room. Laurie followed, pausing briefly by Nelson's desk to ask him to reschedule as many of her afternoon appointments as he could.

She gave a couple of final instructions to the asthma patient who was still sitting at her desk, and when the child had gone, she turned her attention to the father and daughter again. They looked surprisingly homey, with the unconscious girl ensconced in the big chair and the man sitting on one arm of it, leaning protectively over her.

Laurie liked the way he was watching his daughter. She liked the fact that he'd wanted to afford her some privacy, to protect her from the stares of the strangers in the waiting room. He intrigued her, and it wasn't just professional courtesy that made her say, "I'm Laurie Houston, by the way. And you?"

"Clint Daniels."

He barely bothered to look up. She got just a brief shot of those blue eyes this time, barely enough time to see the agitation in them. The man was pretty deeply stirred up, she realized.

"What makes you so sure your daughter didn't eat lunch today?" she probed.

She liked the way his hand was touching the girl's hair, as if to reassure her even in her unconscious state. "We had a fight about it this morning," he said. "Hell, we have an ongoing fight about every bite she eats. It's the main reason Dr. MacDonald recommended we come to see you. Heather thinks I'm being unfair to her because I won't let her eat the cafeteria food like the other kids do." He rubbed his daughter's shoulder briefly, and his movements reminded Laurie again of a big cat uncharacteristically agreeing to play—roughly, but amiably—with some smaller creature.

"That's a common problem with diabetic kids," she agreed. "Especially if they're diagnosed when they're teens."

"Tell me about it." For a second time there was a glimpse of something between anger and humor in his spectacular blue eyes, and then the expression passed.

The girl moaned again, sounding as though she was closer to consciousness this time, and Clint Daniels looked back down at her. "I'm sorry, honey," he said, and this time the pain in his voice was unmistakable. "I know I'm no good at getting this all across to you, am I?"

"So you think she's been skipping meals, rather than eating what you tell her to?"

"I know she has. Half the time she brings home the lunch I've made her. The rest of the time, I don't know what she does with it. Throws it out, most likely."

Now that the immediate crisis was over and Laurie had time to take a deep breath and calm herself down, she was surprised at the range of emotions that were chasing around inside her. She felt an immediate empathy for this beleaguered father, and a sense of how strong his affection for his daughter was. It showed itself in the way he was smoothing her fine hair back from her pale forehead, easing her gently back into consciousness.

And at the same time, there was a crazy little impulse inside Laurie that had nothing to do with Heather, or diabetes, or sudden surges of adrenaline. Now that she'd had time to look at Clint Daniels more carefully, she found herself liking what she saw in a way that had everything to do with being a woman and very little to do with being a consulting nutritionist.

Something about him was a bit larger than life, she thought. His fingers, strong and blunt. His wide cheekbones, and the solid wall of his chest. Those eyes, direct and uncompromising.

He was a man who knew what he wanted, she thought. And something in his attitude hinted that he usually got it. And yet he was so gentle, waiting for his daughter to open her eyes. She found herself warmed and intrigued by the idea of him, and wanting to know more.

In two minutes the vague intrigue escalated into outright mystery, because once Heather actually *did* open her eyes, Clint Daniels turned into another person entirely.

He'd been massaging her shoulder gently, watching her eyelids flutter, and consoling her in a low voice that resonated pleasantly in Laurie's ears. That voice would lure *me* back out of the darkness, she was thinking, when suddenly the sound of his soothing voice stopped. The silence was deafening.

Laurie felt the beginnings of a frown tugging at her eyebrows. Heather was struggling to focus now, and kneeling down at the foot of the chair Laurie instinctively took over the refrain Clint had abandoned. "You're okay, Heather," she said reassuringly. "Just lie quietly, and wait till you feel better."

As she spoke, she was looking up at Clint. As Heather's eyes opened, he withdrew his comforting hand, and sat up ramrod-straight on the arm of the big recliner. Heather was shaking her head now, as if trying to clear it, and the motion seemed to galvanize Clint into motion. He stood up abruptly, leaving his daughter alone in the chair as he headed for the other side of the office.

He still reminded Laurie of a big cat, but now it was caged, penned up and unwilling to lose its dignity by rattling the bars. She watched him pace up and down the length of her small office, and frowned more deeply as she took one of Heather's cold hands and rubbed it.

"What happened?" the girl asked, and Laurie paused, giving Clint the chance to answer his daughter's question if he chose to.

He didn't. His pacing was virtually silent, and single-minded.

"You had an insulin reaction," Laurie said matter-of-factly. "I'm Laurie Houston, the nutritionist you were coming to see. You passed out in my office. But you're going to be okay now, if you just take things slowly. Your father's here," she added, looking up at Clint. Surely now he'd take the cue to offer his daughter some reassuring words, as he had done only a few minutes ago.

But again, he didn't follow Laurie's lead. Thoroughly puzzled now, Laurie decided to push a little harder. "He was very concerned about you, Heather," she said, raising her voice to make it clear to Clint that she was talking to him, too.

"Yeah, I'm sure."

Heather's soft answer held a tired disbelief. Laurie frowned again, even more puzzled. What was going on here? One moment Clint Daniels had been a loving parent, and now he'd withdrawn into total silence.

The silence ended abruptly when he reached the far end of the office and turned to look at his daughter. "Did you eat your lunch?" he asked.

His tone wasn't particularly angry, or accusatory. Or interested, for that matter, Laurie realized with surprise. It was merely a request for information, posed the way one might ask what time the next bus left from Timmins for Sudbury.

"No." Heather's voice had gotten smaller. Was the girl frightened of him? Laurie couldn't help but wonder. But there was no threat in Clint's manner, just that polite and utterly unexpected distance.

"This has to stop, Heather," he said, and then resumed his pacing.

Laurie wouldn't have blamed him for feeling angry. Any parent coping with a diabetic child had a tough job, and coupled with adolescent rebellion, resistance to a new and difficult diet could be a hard thing to overcome. But Clint Daniels didn't seem angry. He seemed businesslike. He wasn't indifferent, but he wasn't emotionally involved, either.

For the second time that afternoon, Laurie was glad she had her professional training to fall back on. She had grabbed Heather's file when she'd reentered her office, and it still lay on her desk. Giving the girl's thin shoulder a final encouraging squeeze, she moved away from the big chair and sat down at her desk.

"Mr. Daniels," she said crisply. The pointed tone of her voice made him stop pacing, and he turned to look at her. "I'm going to need some medical history on Heather. Why don't we take care of that while she rests a little while longer?"

For two crazy seconds something flared in his blue eyes that made her think he was going to refuse, wash his hands of the whole business and leave the place in the same whirlwind that had brought him in. Then, once again, he seemed to get control over whatever emotions were churning around inside him.

Laurie waited, growing more curious. His eyes were darker around the edges, making his blue stare more intense. What was the reason for that inner anger, and why was he working so hard to keep it from showing?

"Have a seat," she said, indicating the chair opposite her with what she hoped was a casual gesture. She was good at handling medical emergencies, but she *hadn't* had a lot of experience taming wild animals.

Finally, he accepted her invitation. He sat down slowly, watching her the whole time. His gaze was wary, reinforcing her image of him as a predator trapped against his will.

This was crazy, Laurie thought. In two minutes everything would go back to normal, and she'd be dealing with nothing more unusual than a tired parent and a newly diagnosed diabetic teenager. But something told her there was more than that going on here.

The same intuition told her she was already more than professionally involved in it. She remembered the way her heart had gone out to the man as he'd sat at his daughter's side, stroking her hair. And that feeling made her uneasy. One of the rules she lived by was never, ever to get personally involved in a patient's case. It was a rule she'd made early on, when the memory of the way she'd had to play surrogate mother to her two younger brothers was still very fresh in her mind.

She cleared her throat and flipped open the file in front of her. "All I've got here are the bare bones," she said. "I see Heather was diagnosed by Dr. MacDonald about three months ago."

"That's right." Clint Daniels cleared his throat, too, and adjusted his tie. He was the quintessential modern businessman in that navy blue suit, Laurie thought, but the conservative pinstripe, white shirt and dark paisley tie contrasted oddly with the unspoken feelings in his eyes.

"I took Heather to Dr. MacDonald when she started complaining about being tired and thirsty all the time," he went on. "He figured out pretty quickly what was wrong."

Then, he described Heather's initial period of hospitalization and the process they'd gone through to figure out a working insulin dosage for her. Laurie thought he seemed glad to have facts and figures to talk about, but when she was through listening and taking careful notes, she knew she had to press him for some more personal information. She watched closely, wondering how he'd react to her questions.

"Is Heather's mother involved at all?" she asked.

A quick shake of the head. "No. She died two years ago."

Laurie glanced over at the girl. Heather was watching her father with sullen interest.

"I'm sorry," she said. "What happened?"

"She was in a car accident," Clint replied. "Some fool had one too many martinis at happy hour down in Toronto and then got on the highway at rush hour."

He might have been talking about the state of his lawn for all the emotion he showed. Laurie fought a smile, thinking that she knew men who were more passionate about their lawns than Clint Daniels seemed to be about his family. Somehow, though, she couldn't get that first impression of him out of her mind. There had been a hundred emotions behind those blue eyes, all fighting one another.

"Was your wife living with you at the time?" she probed.

"No. We'd been divorced since Heather was three. Heather lived with her mother."

"I see. And you lived here in Timmins." If he'd wanted to put distance between himself and his ex-wife, he'd done it with a vengeance. Timmins was a long way from Toronto.

"No." The blunt monosyllable cut short her conjecturing. "I lived in Toronto, too."

"And Montreal, and Calgary..."

Heather's soft voice surprised them both. They turned to her. "You were never in Toronto for too long," the girl added, looking at her father.

He gave her quick shrug, admitting her point. "I was pretty busy in those days," he said. "I traveled a lot."

Timmins was an odd place for a jet-setting businessman to end up, Laurie thought. Aside from some minor flaws—like its winters—she liked living in the small northern Ontario city. The pace of life here was far from frantic, which suited Laurie just fine, but she had to wonder what had brought Clint Daniels here.

She wanted to ask him, but she sensed that getting too personal might put him even more on edge. Instead, she settled for asking, "And what do you do, Mr. Daniels?"

"I gamble."

Laurie blinked. "You mean horseracing and slot machines?" That didn't go at all with the stylishly tailored blue suit and his general air of self-control.

"No." A faint smile flickered in his eyes. "No, I buy up companies that don't work. And then I gamble a lot of capital so that I can make them work better."

"And do you usually succeed?"

This conversation was way off the track, Laurie knew. She should be talking about carbohydrates, not investment capital. She rationalized her interest, briefly, by telling herself that she needed a complete picture of Heather's home life before she could really help the girl.

"Usually, yes." The hint of a smile was still there. Talking about business made him feel safe, Laurie realized. Talking about his daughter seemed to scare the stuffing out of him.

She made a couple of quick notes, thinking how little the facts seemed to reflect the man in front of her. "Father a successful investor," she scribbled, in the handwriting that her friend George MacDonald had often told her was messy enough to be a doctor's. "Mother dead two years, car crash. Heather lived with mother from age three to thirteen."

She gave the girl another quick look. Heather's eyes were closed again, as if she'd withdrawn from the whole scene. Laurie wanted to ask a dozen different questions: Had Heather been happy with her mother? Was she happy with her father? What were Clint Daniels's feelings about suddenly finding himself responsible for a thirteen-year-old daughter? Was resentment one of the things Laurie had seen seething in his blue eyes?

Asking those blunt questions would get her nowhere, she knew. She reined in her own curiosity and went back to the basics.

"So three months ago Heather was diagnosed as having insulin-dependent diabetes," she said. "I assume Dr. MacDonald set out a diet for you to follow."

"He explained the principles of the diet," Clint said. "And I've been trying to get Heather to stick to it, but—" He hesitated, as if in spite of his own frustration, he didn't want to criticize his daughter in front of a near-stranger. "We're having some problems with it," he concluded. Heather had opened her eyes again and the look that passed between Clint and his daughter was far from friendly.

"It's not easy to get used to a big change in your diet, Heather," Laurie said. "Everybody has problems with it at first."

"He's always making me eat when I'm not hungry," Heather said accusingly. "And I can't eat any of the stuff my friends eat."

"The diabetes diet can be a tough one, all right," Laurie said.

"And he says I have to exercise," Heather went on. Laurie's sympathetic smile seemed to have opened the floodgates; it was as though Heather had just been waiting for someone to unload on. "I hate exercising, especially that stupid exercise bike."

"You exercise at home?"

"We work out three times a week," Clint broke in. From the looks of his broad shoulders and the effortless way he moved, he worked out more than that, Laurie thought. But his answer intrigued her.

"Does 'we' mean you work out together?" she asked.

"Yes. I'm not asking Heather to do anything on her own."

"Including the diet?"

"Including the diet. I stick to it as well, when we're eating together. Hell, one of the books I read even suggested I learn to inject myself, with saline solution, so I've done that." There was a rough rasp of anger in his voice again, despite his attempt to suppress it. "Although I've done everything that's been suggested to deal with this thing, it feels as if we're getting nowhere. She still throws her lunch away and ends up making herself feel worse."

He leveled his gaze at his daughter, and Laurie saw the girl recoil a little under its thousand-watt blaze. "It's a lucky thing you happened to be in Ms. Houston's office when you had this reaction," he said. "What if you'd been somewhere else?"

For a moment Laurie had heard an echo of a normal parent's anger in his voice, anger that was rooted in concern and affection. But it disappeared as quickly as it had surfaced, and that businesslike demeanor took over again.

"Dr. MacDonald suggested you might know some techniques for making the diet more flexible," he said curtly, turning back to Laurie. "Frankly, I was a little surprised that he suggested seeing a nutritionist. I thought diabetes was something a doctor usually handled."

She saw the challenge in those bright blue eyes. He was questioning her credentials, she realized, and her spine stiffened slightly in response.

"You'd be surprised at the things nutritionists are called upon to handle," she said, her tone crisply professional now. "*And* at the number of things that are affected by diet. I have several patients with asthma who were constantly running back and forth to the hospital to visit the oxygen tent before they changed their diets."

He was skeptical but interested, she could tell, and she went on, willing herself not to become defensive just because a handsome and overbearing stranger was unfamiliar with her line of work.

"I see a lot of people with food allergies, which are far more common than most people realize," she went on. "And, of course, there are all kinds of special diets pertaining to heart disease and high blood pressure, as well as diabetes and any number of other conditions."

Had she passed his test? She couldn't tell. "And to think I thought a nutritionist was someone who just told you to eat your vegetables and watch your weight," he said.

"I think you're confusing me with the school nurse you remember from high school," she told him.

An odd look crossed his face at that. His tone, which had been pleasant and interested, hardened again. "Believe me, my school nurse looked nothing like you," he said. He went on quickly, as if he'd said more than he'd meant to. "All right, now that I understand why Dr. MacDonald wanted us to see you, what information can you give me to make things work better for Heather?"

No wonder Heather had wilted under his frown, Laurie thought. There was a powerful strength of will in those eyes, and she felt the full force of it herself. She searched for a tactful way to suggest that he was going about this the wrong way.

"I can give you lots of information," she said slowly, "but it sounds as though you've already done a lot of reading on your own."

"He made the library special-order every book on diabetes in the country," Heather put in, and Laurie was heartened to see a sudden gleam of humor in the girl's brown eyes. Heather, at least, was approachable.

She wasn't so sure about Heather's father. He was still frowning, his sandy eyebrows lowered at both of them. "I believe in getting all the information available, and *then* making my decisions," he said.

"That's very wise," Laurie told him, "but there's more to this kind of situation than just getting information."

He was looking wary again, as though he wasn't sure he wanted to know what else was involved. Finally, though, he asked, "What do you mean?"

"I mean that, for better or worse, you and Heather are partners in this. You need to find a way to work together, just as much as you need to find a diet that works, or an insulin dosage that keeps her blood-sugar levels stable.''

His frown deepened. ''As I've already told you, we've tried,'' he said bluntly. ''It hasn't worked. That's why we're here.''

He obviously doesn't like admitting defeat, Laurie thought. ''The past few months have probably seemed like forever,'' she said gently, ''but believe me, in terms of coming to grips with Heather's condition, three months is not a long time. Now, if the three of us start to work together—''

She'd underestimated just how wary he was. He seemed to take her words as a signal that she was about to go too far. He got to his feet in an instant, and Laurie realized that those powerful muscles must have been coiled as tensely as those of a waiting cat ready to pounce.

''That's not what I had in mind,'' he told her. ''I came today because I wanted to give you what background I could. But from now on it's going to be Heather's job to meet with you, until she accepts that what I've been telling her about her diabetes is true.''

Laurie didn't like being loomed over, so she stood up, too. He still had a good five inches on her—he was at least six-one—and his broad chest made him seem even bigger. Still, she managed to hold her eyes steady with his as she said, ''It sounds as though you're trying to cut Heather adrift, Mr. Daniels.''

''Believe me, that's the last thing I'm trying to do.''

Again the conflicting mix of emotions in his blue eyes brought her up short. She frowned. ''Then why are you so eager to send her to me on her own?'' she asked. ''Why not come with her?''

He raised his big hands in the air, then let them drop to his sides. There was something both angry and defensive in the gesture.

"Have you even been in a maze, Ms. Houston?" he asked.

"I've doodled with some on paper, if that's what you mean."

"I'm talking about *real* mazes, the kind they make laboratory rats run around in, only human-sized. When I was in the army, a bunch of us went to an amusement park one night and paid a buck to try to find our way to the other side of one. It had brick walls—must have been a hundred miles of brick."

Laurie waited. He seemed to be choosing his words carefully, skirting around how they made him feel.

"That's what Heather and I have been doing," he said. He looked briefly at his daughter, and then back at Laurie. "We've been chasing around for three months now without getting any closer to figuring out how to tackle this thing."

Laurie looked at the girl. Heather was staring at her interlocked fingers in her lap, mutely confirming what her father was saying.

"I still don't see why Heather's visits here can't include you, too," she said.

Clint Daniels gave an angry sigh. "Because I've done all I can," he said. "I've studied, I've read, I've learned what I could about diabetes. Hell, I dream about it at night. That's how deeply involved I've become. And Heather—"

He seemed on the verge of letting his temper explode. Laurie felt herself leaning forward, almost hoping he'd let himself go. She had a feeling the results might tell her a lot.

He didn't explode. She could see the effort it cost him to rein himself in, and return to that uneasy self-control she'd noticed in him before. The anger was gone now, except for a shadow still flickering in his eyes.

"I've compromised a great deal to accommodate this disease," he said. "And to be perfectly honest with you, Heather still doesn't seem to understand what she's up against. That's why I want her to come to you alone—because I'm hoping you can convince her of things that I haven't been able to."

Laurie still held her pen in her hand. She tapped it against her lower lip thoughtfully.

"And what happens if I work with Heather for a few weeks, and it seems to me then that you need to join us?" she asked.

From the look in his eyes she could tell he wanted to say *no*. She remembered that the girl had suddenly come back into her father's life after he'd had ten years on his own. Was he such a reluctant parent that he couldn't stand the thought of anyone else—even a health professional whose help he needed—witnessing the difficulties he was having with his daughter?

"Then we'll see," he said finally. The coldness in his blue eyes and the stubborn set of that strong jaw might as well have added up to a refusal, Laurie thought. Well, she wasn't about to shortchange this troubled girl just because her father shied away from his feelings like a wild animal who'd just had a whip cracked in its face.

She didn't pursue the subject now. She'd tried very tentatively to tell Clint Daniels she thought he was approaching things the wrong way, and he'd cut her down without hesitation. She'd be wiser to take things slowly, and hope he'd come around.

"All right," she said. Their stances matched: both had crossed their arms over their chests. Laurie uncrossed hers, willing herself to relax. For some reason she didn't comprehend, this blue-eyed cat had gotten under her skin. "I'll see Heather once a week for six weeks," she went on. "And then the three of us will get together to assess our progress. How does that sound?"

"Fine," Daniels said. "I'll see you in six weeks, then."

She found herself wanting to linger over their polite handshake, not just because she was fascinated by the way her own hand felt engulfed in that broad, strong palm of his, but because she needed to know more, to push him until his armor-plated facade gave a little. From the roiling mix of emotions she'd seen in his eyes earlier, she had a sense that his armor might already be weaker than he might like to admit.

"One more question, Mr. Daniels," she said, as Clint and his daughter walked in the direction of her waiting room.

He turned, wary again. "What's that?" he asked.

"Why Timmins?"

Why did his gaze make her breath catch in her throat that way? He didn't look angry now, merely puzzled. "What do you mean?" he asked.

"I mean, why would a high-powered businessman leave the big city to come all the way to Timmins? It's not a very common move to make."

He smiled at her. There were some out-of-use laugh lines at the corners of his eyes that hinted at how a real smile might transform his face, if he let it. But this smile didn't reach those lines, or the blue depths of his eyes.

"It's more common than you might think," he told her. And with that cryptic comment, he ushered his daughter out of her office.

Two

"All right, George, out with it." Laurie perched on a high stool in her favorite sandwich shop and looked across the table at her friend and colleague George MacDonald. "What's the story on Clint Daniels and his daughter?"

George was busy extracting a pickle from his tuna sandwich and didn't answer right away. When he did answer, his words were addressed to the pickle, not to Laurie. "Why can't they ever get my order right?" he asked. "I don't know why you like this place so much, Laurie. It's been two years and they still don't believe me when I say hold the pickle."

"I like it because it's so warm." Laurie grinned at him.

George satisfied himself that there were no more pickles lurking in his sandwich, and took a big bite. "Anyone would think a woman with blood as thin as yours would move to California, not Timmins," he told her, for perhaps the hundredth time.

She often told herself the same thing, especially now, in the dead of winter. This far north, it wasn't unheard of to have snow ten months of the year, and winter was a freezing eternity that left Laurie's feet and hands perpetually chilly. It was no wonder that the cozy little sandwich shop appealed to her, making it her meeting place of choice whenever she and George could grab a lunch date together to talk.

"You're avoiding my question," she told him. "What about Clint Daniels?"

George waited until he'd finished chewing, and then said thoughtfully, "To be honest, the guy puzzled me completely. That's why I sent him on to you."

"Thanks a lot. Spreading the mystery around doesn't make it go away, you know."

"It interests me to hear you use that word."

"What word?"

"Mystery. There's definitely something mysterious about Clinton Daniels, but I'm damned if I can figure out what it is."

"You mean, the way he is with his daughter?" Laurie looked at her coleslaw as though it might divulge Clint's secret. It didn't. "I had the feeling he was going out of his way to keep her from knowing how much he cares about her."

"I sensed that, too. But there's something more going on. I had a feeling I knew him from somewhere, although he swore he'd never met me before."

Unnerving though her encounter with Clint Daniels had been, Laurie had felt no sense of *déjà vu* around him.

"I can't say he looked familiar to me, George," she said. "The thing that puzzles me most now is what to do about Heather."

"How long have you been seeing her?"

"Almost a month. And we've become friends. I think she trusts me, and believes me when I give her advice. But the problem is, the more I talk to her, the more I find out about her father, and the more I want to track him down and shake him till those white teeth of his rattle."

George shot her a sideways smile. With his unruly brown hair and close-trimmed beard, he reminded her of a perpetual medical student. Sometimes it was hard to picture him as a respected practitioner and father of two daughters of his own.

"Mr. Daniels had better watch out," he teased. "When your brown eyes get to glowing that way, and you start flouncing your ponytail around, I know somebody's in trouble." He opened up the second half of his sandwich, checking it carefully for pickles. "This isn't like you, Laurie. Getting so caught up in a patient's private life, I mean."

Laurie knew he was right. And somehow, although George had been her closest friend in Timmins since she'd come here, she wasn't completely comfortable talking about this with him.

"I just feel badly for the girl," she hedged. "Sometimes I can't believe the things she tells me. I said something last week about how she could relax while her father gives her a shot, and suggested that sometimes a quick hug can do more than all the rationalizing in the world. And she looked shocked, and said her father would never hug her."

George looked pensive. His four-year-old twin daughters were the light of his life, constantly badgering their father for hugs and rides on his shoulders.

"I said, 'Not even when you found out you had diabetes?' and she said especially not then. He'd gone out and started buying books about how to deal with it, but it apparently never occurred to him that what that girl needed most in the world right then was a little fatherly reassurance. Can you imagine?"

"Frankly, I can't. But then, I *chose* to be a father. Maybe Daniels chose not to be, and now that he's saddled with it—

and with a diabetic child, to boot—he's just withdrawing from the whole problem.''

"From what Heather says, no parent could possibly be more conscientious about looking after her physical needs, including shots and exercise and all the rest of it. It's just in the affection department that he comes up a big zero." Laurie finished her sandwich, and sighed. "That's what makes me want to shake him."

"It does sound hard on the kid," George agreed. "Especially having lost her mother, and having to move to a new city. Well, that's one of the reasons I sent her to you, Laurie. At least she'll be getting some understanding from someone, even if it's only once a week.'' He raised his eyebrows at her. "Or are you thinking of extending this relationship beyond your office?"

The question startled her. In the back of her mind, she knew she *had* been thinking about it. "You know I don't work that way, George," she said. To her own ears, her words didn't sound completely convincing.

"Not even when there's a mystery involved?"

"I'm a nutritionist, not a detective. And what are you smirking about?"

"I'm just thinking that Clint Daniels seems to have gotten under your skin, that's all."

Laurie felt her cheeks redden slightly. "He's certainly the kind of man who's hard to ignore," she said, choosing her words carefully. "But I'm telling you, George, my interest in him doesn't go an inch beyond the far side of my office door."

It was a fine-sounding statement, but it made it a little difficult for her to explain to herself how she ended up later on that day standing on Clint Daniels's doorstep with a book about diabetes in her hand.

Usually half a mile was enough to do it. Even after a tough day, Clint could feel the tension leaving him as he churned back and forth in the pool, plowing through the water until he'd managed to leave the day's frustrations behind him. He always started out feeling tight, but by the end of a speedy half mile, his legs felt strong and springy as he kicked off the tiled end of the pool at every lap, and his upper body hummed with energy.

Today he got all the way up to a mile before he started feeling like himself again.

He reached the end of the pool and made a racing turn that was almost violent, feeling his bare feet hit the hard tile with a satisfying *thunk*. There were times when he thought he'd have liked to stay in the pool forever, refusing to come up to deal with the way his life had changed in the past four months.

He'd coped with becoming a family man again ten years after thinking he was done with that phase. He'd given his daughter everything he could: a secure home, a decent place to grow up, far away from that questionable crowd she'd hung out with in Toronto.

But now she needed a lot more. And he couldn't provide it. He was just too haunted by his own personal demons.

He came up for air at the other end of the pool, knowing he should be starting to get dinner ready. But he couldn't face it just yet, the constant deadlines, the relentless worrying. What if he didn't keep Heather's diet carefully controlled? What if he gave her too much insulin, or too little? He blinked the water out of his eyes and hauled in a deep breath. He was just about to start one final lap when he heard the doorbell ringing.

He waited. Heather was in her room studying, or presumably studying. He could see her closed door through the living room.

The front doorbell rang again. "Heather!" he called. "Could you get the door?"

There was no answer. She was either ignoring him or—Clint gave her the benefit of the doubt—plugged in to her tape player. Growling a little, he hauled himself out of the pool and grabbed a towel.

"Coming!" he yelled, giving himself a cursory toweling off. He wasn't in any mood to deal with someone trying to sell him something, he thought, wiping the water out of his eyes and heading for the stairs. If there was one thing that got his back up these days, it was someone telling him what he ought to do. Like that woman, Laurie Houston...

The memory was so strong he paused at the foot of the stairs to fight away her image. He'd actually looked forward to that initial trip to the nutritionist's, hoping it would give him the key to keeping Heather's diet on track. But Dr. MacDonald had failed to mention a few things, such as the fact that the nutritionist was an extremely attractive woman, with liquid brown eyes that had watched him almost without blinking the whole time he'd been in her office.

He started up the open staircase. It wasn't just her eyes. It was the way she'd stuck her dainty finger unerringly on his most vulnerable spot. It had rattled him, made him unlike himself this past month. He wished he could get her image out of his mind.

Any hope of doing that vanished when he flung open the door and found her standing on his doorstep.

For the moment Clint forgot he was wearing nothing but swimming trunks, or that he was dripping pool water all over the cold tile floor of the foyer. He even forgot that the floor *was* cold. All he could think about was the way his newly limbered-up muscles tightened again at the sight of Laurie Houston. He told himself it was just tension, but he knew it was something more.

Those liquid brown eyes caught him again, and held him. They spoke to him in a language he wasn't sure he understood. They made him want to learn it.

She stood so calmly, waiting. She was bundled up in a winter coat, but his imagination readily supplied the hidden details of her womanly form. And although she was standing stock-still on his doorstep, he remembered the way she moved, with a kind of compact energy that made her seem to quiver with life even now.

He let out his breath in a rush, unaware until now that he'd been holding it. "Good evening," he said.

She gave him a smile. A dimple made a brief, tantalizing appearance in one cheek. "Good evening, Mr. Daniels," she said, as if his formality amused her. "I hoped I'd find you home."

It must be the blood rushing around after all that exercise, Clint thought. He felt his hand tighten on the door handle. He was actually feeling *good*, just standing there looking at Laurie Houston. As if she'd brought him a present. As if she was the warm breath of spring, three months ahead of schedule.

"Aren't you cold?" she asked him.

"No." He spoke without thinking, answering her smile. "I'm not."

"Well, I am," she said frankly. "Can I come in?"

"Sure." He held the door wider, watched her cross the threshold with that compressed grace she had. He'd been quietly fuming about this woman for almost a month. Why did the sight of her make him feel this way?

"Heather's downstairs," he said, shutting the front door. "I can get her, if you'd like."

"Actually, it's you I came to talk to." She was surveying the house around her, and after a moment she turned back to him. "This is a beautiful place. It looks so small from the front—I had no idea it was this big."

"That was the idea when I designed it," he told her. He explained how the house was set into a hill, so that most of it faced away from the front door, down the open staircase. He was pleased with the way his design had worked. Everything was new, glass, tile and wood shiny and impermeable, but at the same time it managed not to seem cold or sterile. It was a good place for his daughter to live.

The thought of Heather took some of the pleasure out of him. Laurie hadn't brought him anything but more difficulties, he sensed, and the tense fist inside him clenched again. To delay the inevitable moment when she'd get down to business, he said, "Come and see the rest of it. It's down the stairs."

Laurie was as glad of the diversion as he was. She'd arrived at the door planning to deliver a neat little speech, then give him the book and be on her way. But the sight of a wet Greek god in very skimpy red swimming trunks had temporarily done away with her concentration. It was one thing for her to imagine the strength of Clint Daniels's body under a navy blue business suit, but the reality of it, three feet away, had thrown her for a loop. And now, without really meaning to be, she was in his house.

"So you're an architect as well as a gambler," she said, as she followed him down the wide, open staircase. His near-silent footsteps reminded her of her earlier impression of him as a big cat. A panther, maybe. No, a lion. His tawny hair, long on top and shorter at the base of his neck, gave him the right coloring for the image.

"Hardly an architect. Just a guy with a lot of ideas about things, and enough nerve to try to make them real."

"And enough money."

Clint turned briefly, sandy eyebrows raised. "Admittedly, having a lot of money helps when you're trying to get people to do what you want."

"It's too bad that technique doesn't work with daughters, isn't it?"

They were at the bottom of the staircase now. Laurie sensed the big open space of the main floor opening around them, but for the moment her eyes stayed fastened on the nearly naked man in front of her. Her words had had an effect, although she wasn't sure yet what the effect was.

He looked as though someone had snuck up behind him, and he seemed angry with himself for not suspecting it was going to happen. His blue eyes narrowed. "You play hard-ball, don't you?" he said. "Come on. You haven't had the best part of the tour."

So he wasn't going to talk about Heather, at least not yet. Laurie made a show of following his lead as he showed her the open-plan living room, with its pine floor and big fieldstone fireplace. But most of her attention was focused on his evasive manner and—she had to be honest about it—that glorious body.

It was tempting to imagine that he wasn't an entrepreneur after all, but an athlete who'd somehow detoured through Timmins on his way to the Olympics. His thigh muscles looked rock-hard—she'd watched their subtle shifting under his skin as he led the way down the staircase—and Laurie was pretty sure there was a law against the way the wet swimming trunks hugged his lean hips.

The growing twinge of pleasure spread inside her as her eyes traveled upward. She could see the hard ridges of stomach muscle, and could imagine the effort it had taken to build them. His upper body, partly hidden by the towel draped over his shoulders, moved with the inexorable strength of a well-oiled machine.

Even his face had the same strength to it. No, correct that. *Especially* his face. The line of his jaw, his slightly lowered eyebrows as he pointed out the features of the house he'd built, the sweep of his dark blond hair back from his forehead—it all had the power of a clenched fist.

A clenched fist hiding...what? Laurie was sure there were good reasons for everything this man did. And the more she was with him, the more she wanted to know what those reasons were.

She was still grappling with the uneasiness that thought called up, when he turned around and said, "And this room is the real reason I wanted to build this house."

Laurie turned as he did. A long sunroom lay ahead of her, brightly lit in the gloom of an early-winter evening. Lush green plants lined the windows, and a narrow swimming pool ran the length of the room, its surface reflecting the lights above. The water moved slightly, slapping at the tiled sides of the pool.

He had been swimming when she'd arrived, Laurie realized. The image of his broad upper body and slim hips muscling their way through the water made her throat tighten slightly.

She moved forward almost automatically, and took her cold hands out of the pockets of her coat. Her guess had been right: the big sunroom was as warm as a southern beach.

"Well," she said, "I've always thought of Timmins in February as more of a prison sentence than anything else. I certainly didn't expect to find a tropical paradise in the middle of it."

His slight smile actually widened at that. "That's exactly why I built it," he said. "I've always liked to be outside, getting my exercise in the fresh air. But I knew what winter up here was going to be like, so I built in my own outdoors."

Laurie was unable to resist the soft lapping of the pool. She walked to the edge, looking into the softly lit blue water, and said speculatively, "You must have known something about Timmins before you moved here, if you went to this length to take precautions against the winter."

"I looked on a map. It doesn't take a genius to figure out winters are going to be cold this far north in Ontario."

Or to figure out that Clint Daniels wasn't the kind of man to choose where he'd live just by looking on a map, Laurie thought. "You moved here two years ago, right?"

"Right." He'd become taciturn again, looking deep into the sparkling water of the pool.

"A year after Heather came to live with you."

"What are you getting at, Ms. Houston?"

"Please, call me Laurie. And I'm just wondering why you made such a big change in both your lives, that's all."

"Is this something you need to know in order to treat my daughter?"

"Anything I can find out will help me understand her situation better." At least, it *sounded* like a good reason for her own curiosity.

She stood her ground, wondering if he would answer. Apparently he decided her question was a safe one, because he finally said, "My ex-wife thought the earth—no, make that the solar system—revolved around Heather. As a result, I don't think Heather ever heard the word *no* until her mother died and she came to live with me. Unfortunately, one of the things her mother never said no to was Heather's choice of friends. Heather had become a member of a group of well-to-do troublemakers, and I didn't like it."

Laurie considered what he'd said. "And so you moved away," she said.

"Yes. Kids can get into enough trouble with no money, God knows, but when they've got the cash to buy fast cars, and drugs—well, it wasn't the way I wanted to have my daughter growing up, that's all."

Of course it's not all, Laurie thought. But she'd learned by now that pushing him too hard didn't work. "So you stuck a pin in a map and came up with Timmins," she teased him.

He almost smiled, as if he knew where she was leading, and was confident of his ability to deflect her questions if he had to. She liked what the fledgling smile did to his eyes. Without it, they could look hard, almost bleak. But when he smiled, there was something boyish in his face, in spite of the big man's strength that radiated from him.

"Come on," he said abruptly. "I'll show you the rest of the setup."

At the nearer end of the sunroom he pointed out the sauna, whirlpool, shower, and changing area. A set of weight-lifting machines that stood at the other end of the room went a long way toward explaining the finely tuned muscles she could see in his arm as he raised it to point out the features of his personal kingdom.

They weren't the obvious muscles of a man who saw his body merely as window dressing, she thought. He looked as though he knew what hard work was all about.

"I've seen health clubs that weren't this well equipped," she said. "And it's so *warm*."

He smiled at the emphasis she placed on the word *warm*. "You really don't like winter, do you?"

"Not even a little bit. My toes and fingers get cold in September, and they don't thaw until May. Here, see for yourself."

Before Clint could react, she'd reached out a hand toward him, and in his surprise, he took it.

She was right, her hand was cold. It was also soft, delicate, womanly—and, above everything else, friendly. The notion of a spontaneous, friendly gesture like this one was so foreign to Clint's world that it stopped him short.

He knew about the kind of touch ignited by passion, or driven by fury. He felt safe with a businesslike handshake. But a casual touch like Laurie's—especially when it went along with her questioning, wide-open brown eyes—made him feel something vaguely like panic.

And something a lot like desire.

The combination scared the hell out of him. He tightened his hand over her cold fingers—too tightly, from the wince that crossed her pretty face—and abruptly dropped her hand.

He discovered his heart was beating hard, and hoped she didn't notice his excitement. Had she made that gesture for a reason, to test his reaction? She'd been testing him in other ways ever since she'd walked in the door. He had a feeling Laurie Houston was the kind of person who went straight to the heart of the matter.

The woman was dangerous.

She also looked puzzled, as if the way he'd dropped her hand was the last thing she'd expected. She was still smiling, though, as she said lightly, "If I had a room like this, I think I'd be tempted just to hole up in it all winter long."

"There are times when hibernation *does* have a nice ring to it." He couldn't keep the bitterness out of his comment.

Laurie heard it, and was surprised. "You don't strike me as the kind of man who would want to escape from it all," she mused out loud, and saw his blue eyes narrow a little further.

"No?" he said. "And what kind of a man *do* I strike you as?"

He'd phrased the question almost jokingly, but something told Laurie his intent was serious. She considered for a moment before she answered.

"A man who doesn't let his feelings get in the way of his actions," she said at last. "A man who overcomes things that are difficult by plowing right over them as though they weren't there."

She was surprised at her own honesty. But something about Clint seemed to demand candor. And he'd asked the question, after all.

"Am I right?" she pursued, when he didn't answer.

His eyes swept over her, and in spite of his swimming attire and her winter coat, Laurie felt as though she was the nearly naked one, not Clint. "You might be," he said briefly. "Listen, I'm going to get some clothes on. And then I should get Heather's dinner started. Wait here just a minute, and I'll be right back."

And then he was gone, disappearing behind the door of what seemed to be a master bedroom suite off the enormous living room. Laurie blinked as she heard the door close, and wondered if she'd just fantasized the whole encounter. The blue-eyed Greek god who'd materialized at the front door was certainly close enough to every fantasy she'd ever had about the male body, and then some.

She took a step closer to the pool, half-mesmerized by its swaying surface. She could feel the warmth of the sunlamps above, and wished she could slip into a bathing suit and slide into the buoyant caress of the water. She was sure the tiled floor under her feet was heated, too. Her chronically cold toes were actually thawing out as she stood there thinking.

She knew, deep down, that all this warmth had nothing to do with heated floors and sunlamps. It came from inside her, and it was fueled by the thought of Clinton Daniels.

Clint wished his heart rate would slow down, or that his belt buckle would miraculously fasten itself. He hadn't felt this out of control in a long, long time.

The kind of man who doesn't let his feelings get in the way of his actions. She was right, of course. He'd built his life around that very principle.

Then why were his damned feelings making his hands shake this way, so that just fastening his belt was a major project?

He knew why. Somehow, Laurie Houston went too deep. Maybe it was the fact that she was the first woman he'd felt attracted to in what seemed like forever. Maybe it was the way Heather's illness had taxed his reserves, and made him feel he needed and wanted help. He wasn't used to that feeling.

Maybe it was just the bottomless depths of Laurie Houston's brown eyes. He wanted to dive into her, and lose himself in her warmth.

"That's ridiculous," he said out loud, and heard the words echo in his big empty bedroom. *She* was the cold one: she'd pointed it out herself.

And in the simple act of taking his hand she'd upset an equilibrium he'd worked twenty years to attain. Clint thought of her probing questions about why he'd come to Timmins. If she found out why he'd moved back here, she'd be perilously close to knowing why he'd left Timmins in the first place.

The thought of his father, and the scars Clint still bore from his boyhood here, were enough to get him back in control. He would deal with this on his own, the way he'd always dealt with the things that mattered most. And he wouldn't let Laurie Houston slip past any more of his defenses, even if she *did* have eyes as velvety-soft as a summer night.

She wasn't by the pool when he emerged from his bedroom. After a couple of seconds he heard her voice from upstairs. "I'm in the kitchen," she called, and Clint headed up the staircase. "Trust a nutritionist to rifle your cookbook collection the moment your back is turned," she teased, as he reached the top.

"It's not much of a collection," he said. Before his daughter had come to live with him he'd never cooked much. And now most of the books on his kitchen counter were connected with diabetes, not *haute cuisine*.

"For what you're dealing with, I'd say it's pretty comprehensive," she replied. "What's for dinner tonight?"

Briefly he outlined the menu he'd planned. "And I really should get started on it," he said. "If there's one thing I've learned, it's that mealtimes have to be regular." He started pulling things out of the refrigerator, adding, "Not that Heather understands that. She still thinks I'm trying to force her to eat when she's not hungry."

"That's exactly why I came to see you tonight."

Laurie's words brought him up short. She seemed to have the power to do that to him without even trying. It occurred to him that he hadn't really wondered why she was here, until now.

"From what Heather's told me, I think you may be taking too rigid an approach to the diet. There are ways of making it more flexible, without endangering Heather's health, you know."

"That's not what Dr. MacDonald thought."

"George is an excellent doctor. But he's not a specialist in diet. I am. That's why he sent you to me. And I've got another book here that I think you should read." She pulled the book out of her purse and handed it to him. She was smiling again, that deep-rooted smile that made him feel suddenly, illogically warmer. "It's brand-new, so you probably didn't come across it when you were making a clean sweep of every book on diabetes that the Ontario library system had."

He took the book from her. "Thank you," he said, a little stiffly. "Can I pay you for it?"

"No. I've only got one copy, and I want it back. But I know you'd rather read it on your own, so go ahead and do it, and bring it back to me when you're done."

Damn the woman, what was she up to now? He could swear, from the secret smile on her small-boned face, that she was pleased at the idea of giving him something that he'd have to seek her out to return.

"Thanks," he said again. "I appreciate your interest."

But not your way of going about it, he almost added. He wished Laurie could simply have sent the book home with Heather, or stuck it in his mailbox. Dealing with her in person was just too unsettling.

"You know, Clint," she was saying, with that gentle concern that seemed to go straight to the center of his tightly clenched stomach, "there's no reason to feel you have to do all of this without help."

"I'm managing," he said gruffly.

"Are you? I've been wondering about that."

"What do you mean?"

She refused to take the hint in his tone of voice. "Just that from what Heather says, it sounds as though the two of you still aren't working together very well."

"We get by."

"Getting by is not enough, not with a diabetic child. You need real trust, and real affection, and from what I hear—"

She'd just wandered into forbidden territory. He couldn't give Heather the kind of father who inspired trust and affection. She was lucky he could at least offer a reliable and competent father: it was a hell of a lot more than Clint himself had had. And even reliability and competence strained his resources sometimes.

"I didn't realize nutritionists made house calls," he told her.

A funny expression crossed her face at that. "To be honest with you, I usually don't," she said. "But as I said when we first met, you and Heather and I all need to work together on this. And since you wouldn't come to me, I decided to come to you."

There was a strange reluctance in her words, as though in spite of what she was saying, she'd come here against her better judgment. Clint frowned. He was about to repeat his thanks for her interest, and to express his concern with getting Heather's dinner on the table on time, in the hopes that Laurie would take the hint and depart. Then he heard Heather's bedroom door opening. A minute later, his daughter came up the stairs to the kitchen.

He hated to hear the way her feet dragged. His wished he could make her healthy, give her the vitality he remembered from her childhood. More than anything, he wished he could see her face light up with real joy.

And then, all of a sudden, it did, because she'd seen Laurie. "Hi, Laurie," she said, with more animation than she'd shown all week. "What are you doing here?"

"Just loading down your overworked father with some more reading material," Laurie said. "How are you feeling?"

Heather shrugged. "Okay, I guess. Since I took it easy in gym class today, like you suggested, I didn't feel so weak afterward."

"Good. I'm glad to hear it."

Clint had been telling Heather to take it easy in gym class for months, but she'd seemed to take a perverse pleasure in overdoing it and then feeling ill. He frowned, looking from his daughter to the sparkling brown-eyed woman who'd dropped into their lives.

Laurie and Heather were chatting about something that had happened at school, relaxed and happy together. Ignoring the fact that two minutes ago he'd wanted Laurie Houston out of his house and at a safe distance, Clint gave in to a snap decision.

"Laurie," he said bluntly, breaking into their conversation, "will you stay for dinner?"

He'd been right about her reluctance. She glanced at the front door, and then at Heather, and he could almost hear her weighing her options. They both felt the same things, he thought with surprise. They were determined to keep at a safe distance from each other, but somehow, something was tugging them together.

It took a few moments, but she finally said, "I'd love to stay for dinner." And Clint's heart lightened ridiculously at the words.

"Be warned—everybody has to help with the dishes around here," he added brusquely, to cover up his unexpected pleasure. He turned back to the fridge to look for the chicken breasts he'd bought the day before. He was already having to admit to himself that Laurie Houston acted on him in ways he couldn't begin to explain.

Three

———

He watched her as they ate the dinner he'd cooked.

There was something about her that made him think of the whole being more than the sum of its parts. She was a pretty woman, there was no denying it. Her dark brown hair, pulled back in a ponytail, was rich and thick. Her skin was flawless, smooth and very slightly olive-hued. Those endlessly deep brown eyes had drawn him in the moment he'd set eyes on her. Her lips were soft and kissable, and when she smiled...

The smile was what did it. He watched her laughing at something Heather had said, and felt the fist inside him unclench a little. The dimples that showed when she smiled were an invitation to smile back. Her smile made those brown eyes flash in a way that made Clint think of blue skies and forever.

He'd never thought in terms of forever. Just grappling with the present had always been enough for him.

He was fascinated by her. If she'd been a candle, he'd have found warmth in cupping his hands around her. If she'd been a spring, he'd have kneeled by her to slake his thirst.

He thought he must be coming unhinged. Clint Daniels, self-made businessman, simply did *not* think this way. He cleared the tightness in his throat, grateful that the sound was lost in the clinking of dishes.

"That was delicious, Clint," Laurie said, wondering why he'd been so quiet during the meal. "Did somebody take you in hand when you were young and teach you how to cook?"

"Actually, it's something I picked up entirely on my own," he said. The crazy image of his own father standing by the stove, whipping up sautéed chicken breasts, almost made him smile. *Almost.* His father hadn't been capable of *standing* much of the time, let alone cooking.

"Well, that just confirms my suspicions about you, then," Laurie continued.

"Which suspicions are those?"

"That you're a man who can do whatever he makes up his mind to do," she said. "Wouldn't you agree, Heather?"

"I guess so." Heather seemed unenthusiastic. "He's good at making money," she added, as if she wanted to say something positive about her father's accomplishments.

"So I gathered." Laurie looked again at the spacious house around her. The kitchen, the first room she'd entered after coming in the front door, was state-of-the-art, spotless and efficient. "I must admit, I'd never thought in terms of wanting to make lots and lots of money, but when I saw that exercise room of yours, Clint, it did make me realize what good things money can sometimes buy."

She was definitely prodding him again, Clint realized. All right, he'd let her think she was unraveling him, if that's what she wanted. "I don't do what I do because of the money," he said slowly.

"Then why?" Laurie thought she already knew.

"The challenge," he said. "The thrill of taking a company that the whole world has given up on, and turning it around."

"The Midas touch," Laurie said thoughtfully.

"I suppose you could call it that."

"And does it always work?"

She couldn't read what was behind his blue-eyed stare. "It has so far," he said. "As I've said, I don't rely on intuition. I get every scrap of information I can lay my hands on before I buy a failing company, and I only lay down my money for it if I'm certain the potential is there for reviving it."

"So it only *seems* like magic to people who haven't done as much work on it as you have."

"Something like that."

He was comfortable talking business, she could tell. She found she didn't want to let him get too comfortable. She'd been more intrigued by him when she'd shaken him up. Talking about Heather had done that, and so had touching him...

Touching him had been like setting her hand on a live wire. She'd felt the jolt of it all the way down to the base of her spine. The sensation of her skin on his had tantalized her, and obviously it had unnerved him. She wanted to know why. She wanted to make him react that way again. She'd realized, the instant their hands had met, that *that* was why she'd given in to the desire to stop by his house today. She'd told herself she'd just stop by and give him the book since it was more or less on her way home anyway. And now she knew that it was really on the way to something much more important.

"Too bad the Midas touch doesn't work in everyday life," she said, and saw his eyebrows lower.

"What's this Midas touch, anyway?" Heather broke in. "You guys are talking in riddles."

"King Midas was a man who was given the gift of turning everything he touched into gold," Laurie explained.

"Like Dad and the companies he invests in, you mean?"

"Yes. But the problem with Midas was that the gift backfired on him. First he found he couldn't eat or drink, because the food turned to gold when he touched it."

Heather giggled, tickled by the idea. Laurie was still watching Clint's face, and the shadow that had crossed it. "That's even worse than having diabetes," Heather said.

"*Much* worse. And the worst part yet was that when his daughter came running to meet him one day, he put his arms around her and *she* turned to gold."

Heather's smile faded. There was a sudden silence around the tile-topped kitchen table, as though the legend of King Midas had just sprung uncomfortably into life for all three of them.

Laurie could hear Clint drawing in a deep breath. "Heather, did you finish your homework?" he asked. That impersonal tone was back.

"Almost," she answered in a small voice.

"Could you finish it now, please?"

"There's something on TV I want to watch."

"Homework first. Then television."

Heather got up, taking her own plate and glass to the dishwasher before she left the room. Laurie stayed seated as Clint cleared the table, watching him. When he'd stacked the dishes in the machine and closed the door with a conspicuous gentleness that made her think he really wanted to slam it, Clint came back to the table and sat down facing her. His eyes had that hard, bleak look that she didn't like one bit.

"Just what are you trying to do?" he demanded.

The question startled her. It was unlike him to be quite so direct. She struggled to come up with an equally direct answer.

"I'm trying to help you and Heather," she said simply.

"By suggesting to her that I'm cursed or something?"

Damn it all, he wanted to shout, *it's nothing but the truth.* But he didn't want Heather to know that.

"I didn't say you were cursed," Laurie pointed out. "I only said—"

"That I reminded you of King Midas, who turned his daughter into cold metal. That sounds pretty darned close to me, lady."

The buried emotions in his voice and his eyes tugged at her. Part of her wanted to stay the hell away. The rest of her couldn't help reaching in his direction, in spite of the barbed warnings in his voice. When he saw her leaning toward him, that uncertainty seeped back into his ice-blue eyes.

"What are you fighting so hard against, Clint?" she asked frankly. "Is it me, because you don't like me interfering?"

For a half second she thought he was going to respond to the way she'd moved closer to him. Then he dragged himself away, up and out of his chair, and started pacing the kitchen the way he'd paced her office the day they had met.

"Just so you know," she went on, "I don't usually do this. Visit my patients at home, I mean."

"Should I be flattered that you're making an exception in this case?"

"That wasn't what I meant. I just didn't want you to think I make a habit of trying to step into other people's personal lives." In fact, she made a habit of *not* doing that very thing. Laurie knew her explanations to Clint were partly an attempt to sort this confusing situation out for herself.

Her admission seemed to interest him. "You're right. I don't like people interfering in my way of doing things," he said slowly.

The sentence didn't sound finished. "But..." she prompted.

"But there's more to it than that."

"Care to tell me what?"

"No, I don't." This time his words held a distinct warning. Laurie changed her tack.

"You know what's kind of funny about this?" she queried.

Clint said "What?" as though he'd be glad to find anything funny at that particular moment.

"I can't remember how the story of King Midas turned out. Can you?"

That stopped his pacing, at least. She saw he was breathing hard, as if he'd been running, or lifting heavy weights. "I was never much good at fairy tales," he said. "I can't remember, either."

"What were you good at?" she asked softly, standing up and coming around to his side of the table.

"When I was a kid, you mean?"

"Yes." She crossed her arms and waited. Earlier that day, she'd wondered if her black woolen pants and auburn wool turtleneck would be warm enough for the frosty February weather. Now, she was feeling almost *too* warm.

Clint seemed to be having the same problem. He'd put on a navy blue flannel shirt and jeans when he'd changed out of his swimming trunks; and now he tugged at the unbuttoned collar of the shirt as though it was too hot for him.

"I was good at staying alive," he said finally. "Good at staying one jump ahead of . . . the authorities."

"Were they after you? The authorities, I mean." She had a feeling he'd been meaning to say something other than "authorities." She wanted to know what it had been.

"You don't let up, do you?"

"I'm curious about you."

"You'll have to stay curious, then."

"I'm more than just curious. I'm intrigued." She pushed away from the table with her hips and moved closer to him. It was exactly like approaching a big cat in a cage. She could almost hear the snarl start in the back of his throat. "I'm attracted, too," she said, more softly now. She felt driven by honesty, and by the charge that ran through her when they were close like this. "I feel as though I need to know more about you, somehow. And every time I try, you shut me out."

She could sense him trying to do it now, trying to keep her at arm's length. Refusing to stay there, she moved even closer to him. Her heartbeat thudded in her ears.

"Are you sure you're not just doing this to get me to eat more vegetables?" he said thickly.

"Come on, Clint. Stop changing the subject. What's bothering you?"

He'd stopped pacing a minute ago. Now she wondered if he'd stopped breathing. He was standing stock-still, glaring at her.

"Earlier, by the pool, when I touched you," she pursued, feeling as though she was rushing in where any right-thinking angel would have refused to tread, "you acted as though I'd pulled a gun or something. I mean, I know my hands were cold, but they weren't all *that* bad."

She couldn't help herself. Behind the anger, behind everything, she could see something lost and alone peering out of his eyes. She was drawn to it, reaching out for it as she raised her hand and touched the side of his face.

"Are they really that cold?" she whispered, and drew her fingertips down the strong line of his cheekbone.

Everything in Clint's life turned over in that instant. The indescribable softness of her caress turned him not into gold, but into flesh and blood. His flesh was warmed all over, and the blood was singing in his ears, telling him to *hold her*, to *touch her*. To *let her into the cold dark places*.

Her fingers were still trailing along his jaw. In a movement so sudden it startled them both, Clint brought up a hand and clasped hers, crushing her fingers against his palm.

"Laurie," he said raggedly, "you don't understand."

"Then make me understand," she breathed.

That wasn't what he'd meant. He'd meant she didn't understand how profoundly her touch affected him, how in one blinding moment he'd felt he might let loose all the buried fears and frustrations of the past thirty-five years. And in the same moment he had shown his need for softness, for gentleness, for someone to hold him when his own strength wasn't enough. He barely knew her, for God's sake. He couldn't unleash that torrent of feeling on her, not yet.

The idea that he might do it at all made his head swim. Her fingers were small and acquiescent in his palm, waiting for him to move. That fine-boned face, with the determined chin that had been driving him crazy, was tilted up to him. Suddenly he knew why Laurie Houston had been haunting his dreams. He wanted her, wanted to lose himself in the warmth of her brown eyes and smiling lips.

"This is crazy," he muttered, teeth clenched, muscles straining against the urge to pull her against him.

She did it for him. With a neat half step she closed the distance between them. "I agree," she said, smiling up at him. "And what's wrong with that?"

Her smile pushed him over the edge. That, and the way her slender body fitted against his, driving every thought out of his head except her softness, her desire to be close to him. Clint had spent most of his life struggling to stay in control. But now he stopped fighting, and just responded.

His arms pulled her to him, hands feeling the soft resilience of her skin through her sweater. The hunger he felt was immediate and overwhelming. "Laurie," he said, his voice came out not sounding like his own. Her name hung in the supercharged air between them, until he swept it away with his kiss.

Laurie felt his strong fingers splayed across her back, imprinting her with their mark. She'd seen the torrent building in his eyes, but that hadn't prepared her for this fierce embrace, or the sound of her name on his lips. It sounded urgent. It sounded desperate. She raised her arms to encircle his neck, caught up in his desperation.

His kiss didn't even pretend to be subtle. His mouth captured hers roughly, and Laurie heard the buried moan that came from deep in her throat as her lips parted to meet his. She had barely enough rational thought left to marvel at how long she seemed to have been wanting this: the unbridled need of this strong man, the way his lips felt against hers and the clean, male scent that swam in all her senses. That tiny, rational part of her identified it as mostly swimming pool. The rest of her dug deeper, and drank in the warm, earthy perfume that was wholly Clint.

Her tongue met his, matching his need. There was so much more than simple desire in the kiss, although desire was there, too, pounding deep inside her. But a need to break down this mystery man's defenses added a vivid coloring to the pulse of physical hunger she felt for him. As his hands roved over her body, exploring her curves through her wool sweater and trousers, she couldn't stop imagining how this barely hidden hunger would feel if they ever let it evolve into full-blown lovemaking. She felt buffeted by the very idea of it.

She heard him utter an abrupt groan that might have been an attempt to regain the control that had vanished at her touch. His kiss softened. For a long moment he explored her mouth with a gentleness that seemed to have regret, and a hint of finality, in it.

Laurie found that his gentleness affected her even more than his fierce passion had. The pulsing inside her spread until every part of her was filled with it. She raised herself on tiptoe, eyes tightly closed, following the delicate tracings of his tongue against the warm interior of her mouth.

She felt him run a hand over her hair, and take in a long, quivering breath. Then, just as he lifted his lips from hers and seemed about to let her go, he pulled her even more closely against him.

The gesture was the most surprising thing yet. He'd rebuffed her, told her to stay out of his business, shocked her at his response to her touch. And now he'd ignited a smoldering desire that she knew was going to haunt her for a long time. But this—this was something different.

It was a simple need for human contact, for warmth and reassurance. It was a *hug*, for heaven's sake.

Startled and glad, Laurie hugged him back. They held each other tightly, locking their bodies together. Desire was still coursing through Laurie's veins, but for the moment all that mattered was that Clint was holding onto her as though he never wanted to let her go.

He did, finally. She could feel the shuddering in his muscles as he released her, and the two of them stepped apart. Laurie wondered if everything she was feeling showed in her eyes. She didn't think she could hide the passionate exhilaration that was coursing through her.

Exhilaration seemed to be the last thing on Clint's mind. He was moving slowly, almost heavily. His movements were nothing like the lightning-like way he'd captured her in his arms, or the sure, strong caresses that had made her feel so ridiculously light-headed.

Did he regret having let himself go this way? Laurie waited, without speaking. She wanted to hear what he had to say.

He leaned against the kitchen counter, arms across his chest as though he could slow his breathing that way. Laurie was breathing hard, too, and the sight of Clint's masculine collarbone, rising and falling under the open neck of his dark blue shirt, did nothing to calm her down. She'd felt caught up in a whirlwind while he'd been holding her. Now she wanted to be back in his arms, finding out what her fingers would feel like running along the base of his neck, trailing across the outlines of that broad, powerful chest.

His hair had been thick and soft between her fingers. She wanted to touch every part of him, to hear him gasp out his startled need again.

She shook her head slightly, as if trying to chase those troublesome images away. At the same moment, Clint spoke.

"It's been a long time since I held a woman that way," he said slowly.

She smiled at him. "At least you haven't forgotten how," she said. Part of her flippancy came from the bubbling well of feelings she couldn't and didn't want to suppress. Part of it came from a desire to keep him off his guard.

It worked. Clint frowned. "To be honest, I'm not sure I *ever* held a woman in just that way," he said. The words seemed involuntary, as though she'd put him under a spell to make him tell the naked truth.

"Not Heather's mother?"

He drew in another long breath, and he regained a semblance of control. "There was never any real passion between Heather's mother and me," he said. "She wanted a home and a family. I was a convenient way of getting those."

"And were you expendable, once she'd gotten them?" Laurie remembered that his marriage hadn't lasted long.

"Not exactly. It was more that she thought she'd married a responsible career man. When I started playing around with investing and taking changes, my wife thought I was risking our security. She couldn't deal with it."

"So she left and took Heather with her."

"Yes."

Laurie wished she could think more clearly. There were things she wanted to ask Clint, things that she needed to know. "Did you miss your daughter when she was gone?" she asked softly.

She'd expected him to start pacing again, but he didn't. He stayed rooted in one spot, next to the dishwasher. "Part of me did," he said finally. "But for the most part I was taken up with business and traveling. Since my wife had always taken care of the baby by herself, there wasn't even a real change in my routine with Heather gone." He shook his tawny head, and Laurie was reminded of the potent scent of his hair, filling her nostrils. "Doesn't sound very fatherly, does it?" he said ruefully.

"Maybe not, but it does sound understandable, if that's any consolation."

The word brought a new wariness into his handsome face. "I'm not looking for consolation," he said abruptly.

Laurie remembered the way they'd clung together, and the need in his kisses. She couldn't have been wrong about that, she thought. It was obvious that consolation was exactly what he was looking for. It was just as obvious that he wouldn't admit it, or at least not yet.

His next words made his reluctance to be honest with himself abundantly clear. "All I'm looking for is someone to help me out with Heather's problem," he said. "I didn't mean to get carried away like that."

She wasn't about to let him off so easily. "Which problem?" she said.

"Her diabetes, of course."

"Oh." Laurie leveled a stare at him. "I thought you might mean the problem of why the two of you don't seem to get along."

"I've told you, we get along all right."

"And I've told you, 'all right' is not enough in this case. She needs more from you right now, Clint. Can't you understand what she's going through?" Laurie couldn't believe she was saying the words. This was inviting trouble, she knew. And at the same time, she knew she had to go on. "Heather lost her mother, who adored her," she said. "Then she had to move away from her friends to a very different setting. She's depressed to begin with and then she finds out she's got diabetes, which means her moods swing every which way for no reason she can understand, and she can't eat what her friends eat or do the things they do—''

He cut her off. "Heather's not the only kid to have a difficult childhood," he said. "She'll survive it—lots of people do."

"Were you one of them?" It was time to get some real answers here. The cool and distant look in his eyes bothered her in a very personal way.

"Does it matter?" She could sense him retreating, and it made her want to throw something at him.

"Of course it matters. At a rough guess, I'd say something bad happened to you in your childhood, and you're still letting it color your life. For heaven's sake, can't you see what it's doing to your relationship with Heather? That girl needs more from you, Clint."

She'd expected a flat denial, or a blunt dismissal. Instead, he gave a snort of barely amused laughter and repeated her words, "Something bad..."

She watched him through narrowed eyes. "Worse than bad?" she guessed.

He shook his head, as if he had just woken up. "It doesn't matter," he said.

How could she persuade him that it *did* matter, that being strong and stoical were all very well for himself, but they were causing a lot of pain to his fifteen-year-old daughter? She was trying to frame an answer when she heard Heather clattering up the stairs behind them.

"I'm done with my homework," she announced breezily. "So it's TV time, right?"

"Right." Her father's blunt answer seemed to take the edge off the girl's good mood.

"There's a really good movie on," she said, turning to Laurie. "Want to stay and watch it with me?"

"I wish I could," Laurie said. "But I promised myself I was going to get some things done this evening, and I've already stayed later than I had intended."

She hated to see the disappointed look on Heather's face. But a sudden memory overwhelmed her, of the way she'd felt until she'd left her father's home. She'd been the sole emotional support of her two brothers, called on for everything from bad dreams at midnight to popcorn-making when there was something good on TV. She liked Heather, and she was strongly attracted to Clint, but there was no way she was going to walk into another substitute-mom situation.

"Maybe your father will want to watch the movie with you." Laurie wasn't sure what had prompted her to make that suggestion. *Come on, Clint*, she wanted to say. *Let her know you're in there.*

He didn't even have the grace to offer an excuse. "I'm not interested in the kind of movies Heather likes to watch," he said curtly.

"All my friends like the same kinds of movies," the girl said, petulant now. "You should let me go to their houses, if you don't want my movies playing in your house."

"That's not what I said. You're welcome to watch the movie. I just don't want to watch it with you. And you remember what happened the last time you went over to someone's house to watch a movie."

Heather was looking down at the kitchen floor as though the tile pattern was suddenly very absorbing. "Yeah, I remember," she muttered.

"What happened?" Laurie asked.

When Heather didn't answer, Clint said, "Her friends were eating candy bars, and Heather couldn't resist the temptation. She missed three days of school after that episode."

Laurie had to work to suppress a sigh. There wasn't any hint of anger in Clint's tone, no accusation. It was just that cold, mechanical stating of facts, as though his idea of parenting had been loaded into him like a computer program. Heather probably would have welcomed some anger, she thought. Something—anything—but that deadly calm.

"Yeah, well," the girl said, heading for the stairs again, "I guess I'll go watch the movie, then."

What was Clint thinking, as he watched Heather dragging her feet down the staircase? Laurie felt her lips purse into an annoyed line, and wondered what it would take to convince him how wrong his whole approach was.

He didn't give her the chance to figure it out. "I'll read the book and get it back to you," he said when Laurie turned to face him again. "And Heather will see you as usual on Thursday. Thanks for coming by."

He acted as if nothing had happened but the dropping off of a book, Laurie thought in amazement. As if he hadn't released that white-hot streak of passion that had seared both of them so they could barely catch their breaths.

She couldn't let him get away with it. There was too much going on here, just below the surface. "I'll look forward to continuing our conversation when I see you again," she said, and saw that catlike watchfulness in his eyes.

"Maybe it would be better if you would learn when to let a subject drop," he said slowly.

She made herself smile, shaking her head at him with an impudence that he seemed to call up in her. "You underestimate me, Mr. Daniels," she said.

"I don't think so." His deep voice was a rasp now, the hunger she'd seen in his eyes only a few minutes ago a thousand miles away. "Just be careful *you* don't underestimate *me*."

Then he led the way to the door, and Laurie had to acknowledge that whether she liked it or not, he had won this round. This was a strong, complex man she was dealing with, and one who might very well lock himself up tighter than ever, now that he'd let loose this once.

Outside, it was still February. Laurie shivered as she stepped out the door. "I'd forgotten how cold it was," she said, turning back to Clint almost accusingly.

His eyes were almost as cold as the night air. "It doesn't get any warmer just because you wish it would," he said. She took the memory of his words away with her, and knew it was already too late to back away from this, even if she wanted to.

Four

—

"Any luck with the electrician, Nelson?" Laurie came out of her office rubbing her cold hands together, and looking hopefully at her secretary.

Nelson shook his head. "Sorry," he said. "I've left two more messages with his service, but he's still out on a call. They say it's an emergency."

"It'll be an emergency here, too, if I freeze solid," Laurie said ruefully. "I can see the headlines in the tabloids: Nutritionist Found in Block of Ice. Experts Puzzled."

Nelson laughed. "Put your mittens on," he suggested. "And by the way, it's not as cold as you think it is."

"That's because you're young," Laurie grumbled. "Wait till *you* get to be twenty-eight, and see how your old bones react to the heat going off in February."

A freak ice storm the night before had swamped her electrician with emergency calls, and coincidentally, the baseboard heater in her office had chosen this morning to quit. Nelson and the patients she'd seen so far that day had been good-natured about the chill, but Laurie had been cold to start with, and she wasn't getting any warmer... or any more stoical.

"Who have I got scheduled for the rest of the day, Nelson?" she asked, shoving her hands into the pockets of her forest green corduroy shirtdress. Nelson consulted the appointment book.

"Well, there's Heather Daniels's regular appointment at three-thirty, and then the Schneider twins at four."

It was just two-thirty now. She could easily run home and put on the long underwear she usually wore only for skiing, and a pair of warm trousers, and still be back here in time to see Heather at three-thirty. She was still standing by Nelson's desk, trying to face the idea of going back outside, where it was even colder, when the waiting-room door opened and George MacDonald stuck his tousled head through the crack.

"Is the doctor in?" he asked.

"Barely," Laurie said, waving him inside. "Know any quickie remedies for frostbite, George?"

George raised an eyebrow at Nelson, who said, "The heat's off and she thinks she'll turn into a pillar of ice."

"Ah." George nodded. "The curse of the thin-blooded easterner. I tell you, Laurie, they're crying out for nutritionists in California."

"Don't tempt me," she said. "If my hands were halfway functional, I'd pack up and go right now. What brings you out in the middle of the afternoon?"

"I'm trying a radical new concept. It's called 'a day off with my family once a week.' I'm on my way home to test the concept right now."

"George, it's two-thirty already."

He looked sheepish. "So I had to run in and take care of a few things at the office. As I said, it's still a new concept. Anyway, I thought I'd drop by because something that you might be interested in occurred to me."

He followed Laurie into her office and took the chair opposite her when she sat down at her desk. "It's about Clint Daniels," he said, and then paused to wave an ungloved hand in the air. "This is cold?" he said. "I keep my house at this temperature."

"I pity your little girls," Laurie said, grinning at him. "What about Clint Daniels?"

"Cold temperatures keep 'em sharp," George said, grinning back. "I don't want them getting lethargic."

"Lethargic" made her think of Heather, and that made her think of Clint. The truth was, far too many things had been making her think of Clint in the three days since she'd gone to his house. Hearing George say his name had been like applying another little bit of current to an already humming wire.

George made a great show of taking off his other glove, then his wool hat. Laurie waited, her impatience growing.

Finally, George said, "Well, this is weird, but I think I've figured out how I know Clint Daniels."

Laurie sat up a little straighter. For the first time that day the cold seemed to recede in importance. She'd been wondering about George's feeling that he'd met Clint before, and had come to the conclusion that there must be something to it: Clint wasn't a man you could either forget or easily mistake for anyone else.

"When I was in high school here, there was a kid a couple of years ahead of me named Lindstrom," George said. "A real tough kid, came from out in the country somewhere. I don't remember much about him, other than hearing his father was a pretty tough case, too."

"Tough in what way?" Laurie was barely aware of leaning forward, hands clasped in front of her the way she did when she was giving her undivided attention to a patient's problem.

"I can't remember. What I *do* remember is that when he was about sixteen, Lindstrom just disappeared. One day he was in school, and the next, *poof!* I don't think I ever saw him again. And when Clint Daniels brought his daughter in to see me that first time, and I found myself thinking I'd met him before, Lindstrom must have been the person I was thinking of. Daniel Lindstrom, that was the kid's name.''

"And nobody knew why he disappeared?''

"I really don't remember. But if Clint Daniels is really Daniel Lindstrom, it would go a long way toward explaining why a successful venture capitalist like him would settle here, wouldn't it?''

Would it? Laurie wasn't sure. She *was* sure that something traumatic in Clint's childhood had made him deliberately cut himself off from any feeling or emotion associated with it. But if he really was from Timmins, and things had been that bad for him here, why would he have come back?

George was standing up now, putting his hat and gloves back on. "Anyway, since you seemed so interested in the family history, I thought I'd pass that information along, for what it's worth,'' he said.

She thanked him abstractedly, lost in her own thoughts. It was only when he was at the door that she thought to ask, "Could you pin down the time of year when Daniel Lindstrom disappeared?''

"That's easy. It was right before my first prom, so I must have been in tenth grade. I was so overwhelmed by the idea of taking Mary Catherine O'Toole to the prom that it's no wonder I lost track of what happened to Daniel Lindstrom. God, it feels like a hundred years ago, but I guess it was really just 1968.''

"Thanks again. I appreciate your letting me know.''

Her preoccupied expression hadn't escaped George, who made a point of stopping by Nelson's desk and saying, "Keep an eye on her, Nelson. People who are freezing to death often get kind of vague and dreamy, you know.''

Nelson promised to be vigilant, and George left with a wave. Laurie stood at her office door, tapping her lower lip with a pencil until Nelson said, "You awake in there, boss?"

She came back to earth with a start. "More or less," she said. "Listen, I'm going to run a quick errand. I'll be back by three-thirty, if Heather shows up before then."

"All right. I'll keep trying to contact the electrician."

Laurie had almost forgotten about the cold. She shrugged into her coat and hat with her mind still on the long-ago disappearance of a sixteen-year-old named Daniel Lindstrom. She was almost out the door when she remembered something she'd meant to ask Nelson earlier that day, before the broken baseboard heater had claimed her attention.

"You're fresh out of school, Nelson," she said. "Do you remember the story about King Midas?"

"Something about golden apples, wasn't it? No, the golden touch. All I remember is his turning grapes into gold, and then realizing he couldn't eat them."

"Do you remember how the story ends?"

Nelson shook his close-cropped head. "I'm the math whiz, remember? I wasn't very good at English, or history, or whatever subject that story comes under."

Maybe she would have time to swing by the library on her way back, to look up King Midas. Laurie waved a sketchy goodbye to Nelson, and headed for the newspaper office.

She barely made it back, an hour later. It had been miserably cold in the newspaper's storage rooms, and it had taken her longer than she'd anticipated to find what she'd been looking for. She hadn't had time to get to the library, so the ending of "The Midas Touch" still eluded her. But she'd found something else, something that explained at least the beginning of Clint Daniels's story.

She'd copied down the brief news story in her character-istic scribble, but she doubted she'd need to refer to it again; the details were few and easy to remember.

The article had been sandwiched in between a descrip-tion of the dresses the girls of the graduating class had worn to the prom and an ad for used cars. Youth Hospitalized, the headline said, and the story that followed described a local sixteen-year-old, name withheld, who'd arrived in the emergency room of the local hospital so badly beaten he'd ended up in intensive care. It was briefly mentioned that the police were looking for the boy's father, and there was a hint that the father might have been responsible for the beating.

A very bald story, but as she'd read it, Laurie's fingers had been shaken by far more than just the cold. She'd worked in the emergency room; she'd seen drunks and car accident victims and the grisly results of barroom brawls on Friday nights. She'd always been cool and competent about the blood and the bruises, but the sheer ugliness of what damage one person could inflict on another was some-thing she'd never come to terms with.

Clint. Dear God, what had happened to him? She had no doubt that Clint and Daniel Lindstrom and the youth in the newspaper story were one and the same. The thought of what he must have gone through, lying in the antiseptic glare of the emergency room, beaten by his own father, wrenched at her.

She'd searched the next few days' papers, hoping to find some mention of what had happened next. But evidently no charges had been laid, and the story wasn't followed up. And a sixteen-year-old boy had dropped out of life in the northern Ontario town of Timmins.

Until two years ago. When he'd come back. Laurie shook her head, pausing outside her waiting-room door while she tried to calm herself down. It didn't make sense. Although she had the clues now, she wasn't sure what to do with them. One thing was certain: if she went into the waiting room looking this distracted, Nelson would think she needed George's professional attention.

Fortunately, he was on the phone when she entered. She could hear him saying, "Well, couldn't you squeeze us in before you go up there?" and decided to let him keep reasoning with the electrician rather than stop to ask for messages as she usually did. She didn't see Heather in the waiting room, so she slipped quietly into her office, glad to have a moment alone.

But apparently she wasn't alone. There was someone rattling around behind her desk. Her first thought was that if the electrician was already here, how could Nelson be talking to him on the phone?

Then the man stood up, and she wondered how she could ever have mistaken that broad pair of shoulders. Clint was standing there, as though she'd materialized him out of her thoughts.

"Clint..." Her voice was uncertain, almost as uncertain as his eyes. She tried again. "Are you meeting Heather here?"

"Heather called me at lunch and said she wanted to audition for a part in the school play. She seemed pretty excited about it, so I said yes."

Laurie searched his face, wondering if his complying with Heather's wishes meant his attitude toward his daughter had softened. Those hard blue eyes weren't giving any information on the subject.

"Anyway, the audition was this afternoon, so I thought I'd better call and cancel her appointment. When I talked to your secretary, he said something about your office being sub-zero—"

Laurie couldn't help smiling. "He's humoring me," she explained. "I'm the only one who's really cold."

"Well, he seemed to take it to heart. So I thought I'd drop by with this."

He stepped around the desk and pointed toward his feet, like a magician revealing an extravagant ending to a trick. Laurie's smile widened. A substantial space heater was plugged into the outlet behind her desk, already radiating heat at a great rate.

"Talk about the Midas touch!" she couldn't help saying. "Clint, you may have saved my life."

He didn't share her smile; he just watched her as she pulled off her mittens and held her cold hands out to the welcome heat. "Do you mind if I ask you a question?" he said.

"Ask away." He could ask a hundred, as long as she could keep soaking up this blessed warm air.

"Why did you move to Timmins, if you hate the cold this much?"

"How do you know I moved here? Maybe I'm a native."

He shook his head authoritatively. "Natives don't complain about the winters the way you do," he told her. "They just grin and bear it."

"You're right. I'm a foreigner, from Nova Scotia."

"Really? Join the club."

Her head whipped around. "But you can't—" she began, and then caught herself. "What part of Nova Scotia?" she asked him. Was it possible she'd been wrong, and had built a dream history for the wrong man?

His faint smile didn't tell her the answer. "I was stationed in Halifax when I was in the army," he said. "On that basis I consider myself an honorary Bluenose."

"So you weren't born there." It was a statement, not a question.

"Not really." His words must have struck him as odd, as they did her, because he added, "I tend to date my life from the day I ran away and joined the army. I don't much care to include what went on before that."

Laurie let out her breath. So she'd been right, after all. "Well," she said, straightening up and extending her now-warm hand to him, "even if you're just honorary, I still have to shake hands with a fellow Nova Scotian."

The first time she'd touched him, she'd had no idea what she was unleashing. This time she knew, and she wanted to know more. She wondered if he'd hesitate, try to back away.

His eyes told her he wanted to touch her. They also flashed with an eagerness that made her wonder if he'd re-lived their kiss as often as she had in the past three days. After a pause that opened like a gulf between them, he reached for her hand and took it in his own.

It was far from a casual handshake. For one thing, their eyes stayed locked together, searching, probing. Laurie could feel the stirrings of desire again as the warmth of his palm against hers spread through her, and that rough strength made her surprise herself with her boldness.

"I'm glad to see you, Clint," she said. "After the other night, I had the feeling you might not want to talk to me again."

"I had that same feeling myself." His voice was a little gruff. "But I had some other feelings, too." He cleared his throat. "In fact, I've never had so many feelings about one damn woman in my life."

The slow smile that spread across her face was more than worth the turmoil his confession had cost him. God, she was perfect—her little pointed chin, the flash of her white teeth, those devastating dimples. She should be required to get a license for dimples like those, he thought. Not to mention that glow in her eyes.

He let go of her hand slowly, almost reluctantly, Laurie thought. Again she sensed that struggle in him, the con-flicting tug of self-reliance against his own need for hu-man warmth. She sat down at her desk, and wondered if he'd really come just to bring the space heater, or if there was more on his mind.

If there was, he was taking his time getting to it. He sat down in the chair opposite her, and Laurie waited out a silence that probably wasn't really as long as it seemed, while he watched her with those brilliant blue eyes. There were a hundred things she wanted to say to him, but it was more important to know what he was thinking, and why he'd come here.

His first words didn't tell her. "That's a very young-looking secretary you have out there," he said.

She blinked at the casual statement. Surely he hadn't just dropped in to chat. "He just graduated from high school last year," she said, playing along. "He's hoping to go to college to get an engineering degree, but his parents don't approve. So he's trying to save the tuition money himself."

Clint raised a tawny eyebrow. "I'm sure you're a very generous employer, but can anybody on a secretary's salary really save that kind of money?" he asked.

"Oh, this isn't his only job. He works on weekends for a caterer, and on the side he has a pet-and-house-sitting business. He's great at it. He looks after my place whenever I'm away, and there's no one I'd trust more."

"So you think he'll get to university eventually." She couldn't tell, from his guarded expression, whether he was skeptical or approving.

"He'll get there. As you pointed out yourself, kids can be pretty resilient when they have to be."

He ignored the gambit. Instead, he was surveying her office. "What about you?" he asked. "Are you ambitious, like Nelson?"

She followed his gaze, seeing her small, tastefully decorated office through his eyes. No doubt it seemed very small-scale, to a man used to buying and selling whole corporations. "Professionally, I'm right where I want to be," she said. "I set my own hours, decide my own workload, and I'm doing what I'm most interested in."

Briefly, she told him about her nurse's training in Toronto, and the job offer that had brought her to Timmins. The salary had been what had tempted her at first; it had been enough to enable her to buy her own small house, not too far from the hospital.

"At first, I thought I'd find it rewarding to work in the emergency room," she said. "You know, helping people in a real crisis, and that sort of thing. But after a while the crises started seeming too, well, too preventable, I guess."

"What do you mean, preventable?"

"Well, let's say, for example, that you hadn't taken Heather's diabetes seriously. Say she kept having seizures, and you had to keep bringing her in to the emergency room. I'd have had to treat her, time and time again, knowing that if I could somehow get to the root of the problem, the emergencies wouldn't happen."

"I see." He stroked his jaw thoughtfully. Laurie felt her concentration straying, tugged by the imagined sensations of running her own fingers along the strong contours of Clint's face just as she had done the other day.

"The same goes for car accidents. I thought of going into alcohol counseling at one time, for just that reason. Or domestic violence." She watched him closely, and thought she could see his heartbeat pick up at the base of his neck, where his open shirt collar revealed a seductive hollow. "I saw so many wives coming in over and over, beaten up by their husbands because the men had gotten drunk on a Friday night. It was such a vicious circle, and so needless."

She thought he wanted to clear his throat, but he didn't do it, as though the sound might give him away. But she heard the slight thickness in his voice as he said, "There are a lot of tough cases around Timmins, especially in the outlying areas. Sometimes I think it's the long dark winter nights that gets to them.''

She pushed him a little more. ''You sound pretty knowledgeable, for a newcomer,'' she said.

He shrugged. He still wore his heavy sheepskin coat, and in it his shoulders looked massive. ''I've lived in places a lot like Timmins,'' he said. ''Believe me, I know what they're like.''

Laurie frowned. Should she lay her cards on the table, and see how he'd react? Clint was such an intensely private man. Would it anger him to find out she'd been trying to solve the mystery of him on her own?

The only times she'd seen him open and unguarded were those times that something had taken him by surprise, and shocked him out of that powerful reserve of his. Maybe if she told him what she'd learned, he'd be so taken aback that he'd let his guard down again.

Or maybe he'd just close up tighter. In any case, Laurie knew she'd rather hear the story from Clint himself. Maybe if he grew to trust her more, he'd tell her. She knew the bare facts, but it was even more important to know the feelings that lay behind them.

''So you left the job at the hospital because you wanted to get to the roots of people's problems,'' he said speculatively.

She knew he was obliquely referring to her ''interference'' in his own life. ''I guess you could put it that way,'' she said. ''My decision to leave the hospital was the result of a combination of factors. My friend George—Dr. MacDonald—was leaving the hospital to set up his own practice, and I knew I'd miss him. And he referred so many patients to me to talk about their nutrition problems that I figured I might as well open my own office, too.''

He was watching her closely. ''You like helping people,'' he said. It wasn't a question.

''Yes. Within limits.''

The effect of his blue-eyed stare was like a battering ram, small but insistent. "And what exactly are those limits?" he asked.

Laurie laced her fingers together and looked down at them, avoiding Clint's piercing eyes. "Well, believe it or not, I prefer to confine my dealings with my patients to this office," she said. She was beginning to wish he'd drop the subject.

Not a chance. "You'll forgive me if I find that hard to believe," he said. "You did show up at my house the other night, after all."

"I know." Laurie didn't want to go into it. "That was a one-time special offer," she added, trying to sound glib. "It won't happen again."

As she said the words, she knew, crazily, that she wanted it to happen again. And something in Clint's face hinted that he wouldn't find her presence in his house unwelcome, either.

"Do you miss Nova Scotia?" he asked unexpectedly.

Laurie smiled. "Sure," she said. "Every once in a while I still find myself trying to catch the smell of the sea."

"And your family?"

"What is this? Twenty Questions?"

"I'm just trying to figure you out," he said. "You're a very mysterious woman, Laurie Houston."

That brought her up short. "*I'm* mysterious?" she said incredulously.

"Very. I had the strangest feeling about you when you were at my house. It was as if you really didn't want to be there, but something had pushed you into coming. You seemed fascinated and reluctant, all at the same time."

So he wasn't just a conjurer of gold, but a reader of minds as well! Laurie hesitated, and then said slowly, "You were asking me about my family."

"Now you're changing the subject."

"No," she replied. "I'm just answering it in a round-about way. My mother died when I was twelve," she went on, looking up at him in time to catch a flash of sympathetic interest in his brilliant blue eyes. "I have two younger brothers, who were eight and five at the time. And my father worked very hard." She watched him balancing the equation. "I got voted into the job of being a parent, without even putting my name on the ballot."

It still wasn't easy for her to talk about it, and Clint seemed to sense that. He wasn't fooled by her attempt at assuming a lighthearted tone. "It can be hell when you have to grow up before you're ready for it," he said.

Laurie found herself nodding, grateful for his understanding. "It wasn't easy," she said. "Not only was my father busy, he was devastated by my mother's death. He never really opened up to anyone after that, and I was the one my brothers turned to—and still turn to—for emotional support."

"It must have been a heavy load." His eyebrows were lowered in concentration. "No wonder you moved so far from home."

"Actually, we all did. Barry and his family live in Toronto, and Ellis is in Vancouver. We're pretty far-flung." She cleared her throat, not wanting to get any deeper into the subject. She'd been put on the spot enough for one day; it was time to turn the tables on him. "What about you, Clint?" she asked. "Any family besides Heather?"

"No."

"You must have had parents at one time," she prompted.

"Everybody has parents at one time," he returned soberly. "I just got rid of mine earlier than most people do."

Don't push it, his tone warned. And a little inner voice was telling Laurie the same thing. Despite her own impatience to know more about him, she knew she'd be wiser to wait, and let him tell her when he was ready to.

A tap on the door reminded her that this was still an ordinary working day. She tended to lose track of time and place when she was around Clint Daniels, as if he could turn ordinary moments into golden ones just with his presence.

"I've got patients waiting for me," she said ruefully, glancing at her watch. "But I'm glad you came by, Clint. I've enjoyed talking with you."

"You're just saying that because of the space heater." He caught her eye and smiled.

"I won't deny the space heater is a big plus. I can almost feel my toes again." She stood up as he did, noticing again how he seemed just a little larger than life, his broad shoulders looming in her small office.

"Then I'm willing to call this a good day's work," he replied, still smiling.

"Where *do* you work?" she asked, suddenly curious.

"I have an office in my house," he said. "And I rent a conference room downtown, when I need one." Her question seemed to surprise him.

"I was just wondering about your clothes," she explained. "The first day I met you, you were dressed to the nines. And today you look—well, casual."

And gorgeous, she might have added. His jeans fit him like nobody's business, and in the well-worn dark shirt and oversized sheepskin coat, he could have passed for some kind of northern cowboy, who'd never seen a FAX machine or a corporate jet in his life.

He sounded amused. "The suit was in honor of a visitor," he explained. "Some guy from Montreal had flown up earlier that day to talk to me about a possible takeover."

"So you had to impress him?"

"I don't generally have to impress people. When you've got the capital and they want it, you can make the rules."

"Then why the suit?"

He turned his palms up, and she was reminded irresistibly of the strength in his hands. "Part of the uniform, I guess," he said. "Dressing the part."

They were at the office door now, standing close together. Laurie still wasn't sure why he'd come here; she only knew she liked being with him, and that she wanted to know more than ever what was behind that handsome facade. The thought tickled her curiosity, the same way the memory of him in the skimpy red swimming trunks made her hum faintly deep inside.

"How's Heather?" she asked, as she opened the door.

"She's fine. She'll be here next week, as usual."

"I'm glad to hear she's auditioning for a part in a play. It's good for her to feel she's not completely cut off from what her friends are doing."

At the mention of Heather, his well of friendliness seemed to dry up and the expression in his eyes hardened. Laurie felt the vague annoyance that his treatment of his daughter always evoked, and she added pointedly, "She's a good kid, Clint. I've been enjoying her visits."

"I suppose you want a family some day."

The blunt statement came out of nowhere. Laurie rocked on her heels, stung by the sudden hardness in his voice. His eyes matched it.

"What makes you suppose that?"

"Just something about you. You're so open with Heather. You're good at getting people to open up to you."

Well, she'd wanted to turn the tables on him, Laurie thought, watching him, but she hadn't expected to succeed this well. Now it was Clint who seemed reluctant, yet fascinated.

"I told you, I had lots of practice, early, at being the one everyone turns to for a shoulder to lean on." She heard the slight hard edge to her own voice. She'd conquered the bitterness long ago, but she hadn't forgotten the lessons she'd learned.

"That doesn't answer my question. Do you want a family of your own?"

"Yes." The answer came straight from her heart, without giving her brain time to edit it. "Yes, under the right circumstances."

"And what would those be?"

It felt strangely as though they were circling each other in a ring, choosing their steps carefully. "It would have to be with the right man," Laurie said. "I had a taste of doing it all on my own, and it's not something I'd choose to do again."

He nodded. The expression on his face was serious, and unreadable. "I thought that's what you'd say," he said.

All these cryptic utterances were making her impatient. "Clint, why did you come here today?" she asked him bluntly. "If you just want my biography, I could have sent it to you in the mail. Why did you come here?" Her voice was softer as she repeated the question.

His big shoulders raised and lowered in a shrug. He was moving away from her now, as though her direct questions were driving him away. "Maybe it was for the same reason you came to my house the other night," he said. "I'm damned if I know the real reason for any of this."

And with that, he was gone, leaving her more mystified than ever. She watched his broad back as he strode through the waiting room and out the door, and it was several seconds before she registered the fact that her next patients were looking expectantly at her, or that Nelson was speaking to her.

"Good news, boss," he said. "The electrician's making this his next call. We'll have heat tomorrow."

It occurred to her that she'd stopped feeling cold some time ago, and it had very little to do with the space heater Clint had brought. "They should bottle that man and use *him* to warm things up," she muttered to herself.

"What's that?" Nelson was looking curiously at her.

"Nothing," she said hastily. "Just thinking out loud."

* * *

She was going to have to start turning her thermostat up at night. If it was turned down too far, it would make bells ring, and then sleep was impossible.

The phone rang for the third time, and finally Laurie jolted into consciousness. She'd been burrowing under her covers, where it was warm, and a part of her knew that answering the phone meant getting out of bed, where it was cold.

She also knew that it was three in the morning, just the right time for a crank call. Or an emergency.

"Yes?" she said groggily into the receiver.

Clint's voice chased away any trace of sleep, and got her adrenaline flowing in a hurry. "Laurie, I don't know what to do," he said. She could hear the edge of panic, and sensed him fighting it. "Heather's hallucinating. I can't make her understand anything."

Laurie was already grabbing clothes as she talked. "It's okay, Clint," she said. "I'm on my way. Is she thrashing around?"

"Yes. I can barely hold her still."

"She's having a seizure. Do you have any glucagon to give her?"

"Any what?" His voice didn't rise in pitch, as another man's might have when faced with the same frightening situation, but she heard the emotion in it straining to break loose.

"Never mind. I'll bring some."

"Should I try to get some sugar into her?"

"Not if she's in seizure. She might choke on it." She zipped up her jeans, not bothering to tuck in her night-gown. Heather's safety was all that mattered now.

"Clint? Try to stay calm. I know that's a tall order, but it's the best thing you can do. Keep her from hurting herself. I'll be there in ten minutes."

"Laurie—"

There was such a plea in his voice that she stopped moving for a moment. "Yes?"

"This scares the hell out of me, Laurie."

If there had been time, she'd have smiled. As it was, she gave a quick nod of her head as she pulled on the nearest pair of socks. "That just proves you're human like the rest of us," she told him. "I'm on my way."

Five

___

For the next half hour Laurie needed every scrap of training and experience she'd managed to accumulate in her years in the emergency room, and then some.

Heather's insulin reaction wasn't the whole problem, although the reaction was severe enough. Laurie thanked her lucky stars that she'd just laid in a supply of glucagon, which would boost Heather's blood-sugar level more quickly and safely than sugar. She'd had it waiting in her office, ready to tell Heather about it at their next meeting. Dashing into her nearby office on her way took only a few extra minutes.

She made it to Clint's house in the ten minutes she'd promised, but when he pulled open the front door for her, she realized from one look in his eyes just what an eternity ten minutes could be.

Neither of them wasted any time. Clint was wearing only pajama bottoms, his feet bare and soundless as he quickly led the way down the stairs. Laurie had put on sneakers, but hadn't bothered to lace them up all the way. The ends of the laces clicked loudly on the tile staircase.

"She's quieter than she was," Clint was saying, as he hurried across the big open living room and into Heather's bedroom. "She's not thrashing as much, anyway."

That wasn't a particularly good sign, Laurie knew, but she didn't say so out loud. Clint was already strained to the breaking point.

"That'll make it easier to give her an injection," she said, forcing herself to sound calm. She pulled the glucagon kit from her handbag and quickly began mixing the liquid with the powder. Damn it, her fingers were shaking! When she'd been an emergency room nurse, she'd stitched up head wounds and set bones for years without allowing shaky hands to get in her way. Did her trembling now have something to do with the urgency radiating from Clint as he sat beside her on the bed? She almost wished she'd told him to wait outside.

Except she knew he wouldn't have done it. And she didn't have the heart to send him out anyway, as she watched him surrounding his daughter's rigid, trembling form with a protective arm. The muscles in that arm, softened to mere outlines by the light of the bedside lamp, looked like warm granite, safe and protecting.

Laurie hauled in a deep breath, and willed herself to be calm as she gave Heather the injection. "When did you notice she was bad?" she asked, hoping to take Clint's mind off the fears he was obviously dwelling on.

It took a moment, but his head finally snapped up to look at her. "I couldn't sleep," he said tersely. "I got up to stretch my legs—sometimes looking at the pool helps calm me down."

She barely registered the fact that this was the first time he'd admitted out loud how tormented he sometimes felt.

"I heard noises from Heather's room," he went on. "I didn't like the sound of it, so I came in. She was crazy,

Laurie. I couldn't make her understand who I was or who she was."

Laurie set the syringe down on the table next to the bed, and kept her eyes watchfully on Heather's white face, waiting for any change. "There's nothing scarier," she said sympathetically. "It's like seeing your child possessed by something from another world."

"That's exactly what it was like." His relief at her understanding made her realize just how badly he'd needed her help. The thought warmed her a little, in spite of her own real worry about Heather.

"How long will that stuff take to kick in?" Clint demanded.

"On average, ten minutes. I'd say a little longer, in this case. She was pretty bad."

"But it will help?"

She looked up at him, and saw the naked fear in his face. "She's not going to die, Clint," she said softly, answering his unspoken words. "Trust me."

"Trust you." There it was again, that harsh, unbelieving tone. Clint gave a snort that told her volumes about his opinion of trust, and then he seemed to soften a little. "Well, I guess I have to trust someone, don't I? I've done a hell of a job coping on my own."

"What did Heather eat for dinner?" Laurie asked him. She needed to force his mind back to facts, and keep him from letting his anger at himself get in the way.

"That's the problem. I don't think she ate anything."

"Did she tell you that?"

"No. She called from a friend's house and said they were going out for dinner after the audition, and could she go along. I made her tell me what she planned to eat and where, and it seemed okay. I figured I could compensate with her insulin dosage tomorrow morning. But then this happened."

"Sounds as though she skipped dinner and was afraid to tell you," Laurie speculated.

"Damn it!" He let his anger explode for an instant, slamming a fist down on the bed and jostling the unconscious girl. The moment he realized what he'd done, he reined in his emotions again, and gave Heather a gentle pat as if to apologize for having disturbed her. "Why can't she just be honest with me?"

"She doesn't know what to do with you," she said gently. "Maybe she was faced with having to eat something she knew wasn't on the diet, and she didn't want to do that because she knew it would make you mad. So she skipped it, and didn't tell you because she knew *that* would make you mad."

His teeth were clenched now, his eyes dark and wild. "I don't get mad at her," he said tightly. "I've worked very hard *not* to get mad at her."

Laurie looked across at him, powerfully aware of her attraction to this man. His face looked younger in the dim light, less distant. Suddenly it was easier to picture him as a sixteen-year-old, as vulnerable and confused as his own daughter must have been tonight.

If only he could use his experience to help her, instead of bottling it up and keeping his distance so relentlessly. Laurie opened her mouth, not quite sure how to say the words. Before she had a chance to speak, however, Heather stirred on the bed beside her, and she was aware of a change in the girl's rigid posture.

"I think it's starting to work already," she said optimistically.

"What is this stuff, anyway?"

Laurie told him, describing the advantages of glucagon for a diabetic person experiencing a severe reaction. Clint listened carefully, and she could picture him taking notes in that razor-sharp brain of his. He seemed to absorb facts like the proverbial sponge, she thought. Too bad he wasn't as receptive when it came to good advice.

"I'm going to put the rest of this in the fridge, in case we need it later," she said, pushing herself off the bed. "I'll be right back."

Alone in the kitchen, she stood for an extra minute gulping air as though she'd been in danger of suffocating. Clint's fear and anger affected her as profoundly as if he were someone she'd known and loved all her life. Somehow, without meaning to, she'd become so deeply involved with him and his daughter that the threat of Heather's seizure had nearly driven away Laurie's professional calm. She waited until her heartbeat had slowed, then gave herself the excuse of tying her sneakers properly to buy a little extra time upstairs, and only then did she go back down to the bedroom.

She paused in the doorway, struck by the picture. Clint was half reclining on the bed, his large shoulders making a arch around his daughter's sleeping form. The light from the small lamp warmed the scene, softening the impression Clint's strength always made on her. Laurie thought no father could have looked more loving, more concerned or protective.

Until Heather woke up. Then, she knew, that loving concern would disappear again, until he was like a man performing parenthood-by-the-book. She frowned slightly as she reentered the room. She was damned if she would stand by and watch that unsettling transformation one more time.

Heather's body was lying more naturally, and Laurie pulled up the disarranged covers. "We'll let her rest for a while," she said. "She should be okay now, but I'll check her blood sugar in half an hour, and see how she's doing."

She held out a hand to Clint, who was watching his daughter's face with a fierce concentration, as if she might vanish the instant he took his eyes off her. "Come on,

Clint," Laurie urged softly. "You need to trust that she'll
be all right."

He seemed unwilling to lift his gaze, but finally he became aware of Laurie's reaching hand. She could see the
muscles shift under his shoulder blades as he raised his
hand to hers, and let her pull him off the bed and lead him
out of the bedroom.

Laurie half closed the door behind them. "There," she
said firmly, keeping hold of Clint's hand. "We'll hear her
if she needs us."

He was clearly unwilling to leave the room, and she had
to keep up a gentle pressure to get him over to the sofa. He
walked like a man in a daze, a big shadow following at her
side.

The sofa faced an empty fireplace, with a wrought iron
log carrier next to it. The carrier was full of logs, and Laurie suggested that building a fire would be a good idea. "I
don't know about you, but I'm feeling chilled."

That brought out a stray gleam of humor in him.
"You're always feeling chilled," he observed, smiling as he
moved automatically to lift a couple of logs and some kin-
dling into the grate.

"I know," Laurie lamented. "My friend George keeps
telling me I should move to California."

"Don't you dare." The customary air of command was
back in his voice. "Not until you've helped me figure out
what to do with Heather."

Laurie settled back into the sofa, amazed. All of a sudden, with no fanfare, he was admitting just how much he
needed help. Or practical help, anyway, she reminded herself sensibly. Would he ever admit he needed help with his
long-buried emotions, as well?

She watched him lighting the fire. As he bent over the
fireplace his broad back looked smooth and touchable in
the light of the two small lamps he'd turned on. The heart
rate Laurie had just calmed so carefully began to acceler-

ate again. All she had to do was lean forward and run her hands over that wide stretch of sinew and muscle, to feel the breathing life inside him . . .

She forced herself to stay still, not wanting to disturb his thoughts. She tried again to take deep breaths, but something in her throat got in the way this time. It tightened into a knot as Clint stood and turned to face her, and she saw in his eyes that he seemed troubled by the same impulses that were sizzling through her.

His words confirmed it. "Twenty minutes ago I'd have said I couldn't possibly think about anything except Heather tonight," he said slowly. "But you're a very distracting woman, Laurie Houston." The smile he so rarely showed appeared as he added, "Especially in that slightly unorthodox outfit."

Laurie gazed down at herself, realizing that she was dressed in her flowered flannel nightgown, her oldest pair of blue jeans, and a mismatched pair of socks, one of them blue, the other a flaming green.

"Thanks," she said, grinning at him. "I like to look snappy whenever I'm called out at three a.m. on an emergency."

His smile dissolved. "I haven't thanked you yet for doing that," he said seriously.

She shook her head at him, and felt the weight of her hair on her shoulders. Her wardrobe wasn't the only thing in disarray, she thought, picturing her sleep-tangled hair. "No need to thank me," she said lightly. "I told you how fond I am of Heather. I'm glad I could help."

He rubbed a tired hand over his jaw as he watched her, feeling the slight stubble on his chin. Laurie looked like an angel, he thought, with her dark brown hair tousled like that and her eyes shining, reflecting the light of the fire as the logs started to burn. He felt some of his tension subside just looking at her.

He liked the way the light-colored flannel nightgown made her eyes seem even darker and warmer. He liked the near innocence of her frayed jeans, and that crazily colorful pair of socks. He'd always found her attractive, but it seemed to him that she'd never looked more beautiful than she did now, curled up in one corner of his sofa and looking up at him with such an open expression in her lovely eyes.

On the other hand, he felt a little underdressed in his pajama bottoms, and wondered why it should bother him. It hadn't bothered him to have her see him in his swimming trunks the other day. Was it because he'd felt in control then, certain of himself, and now he was all at sea? In any case...

"I think I'll go put some more clothes on," he said quickly, but she held out a hand to him before he could leave the room. He was powerless against that simple gesture, that spontaneous offer of her touch, of her acceptance.

"Don't," she said. "Unless you're cold, that is."

"I'm not cold."

"Then don't run around making more things for yourself to do. Come and sit down, and try to relax. You've had a tough night."

You said it, he thought. It had been a tough night even before Heather's seizure. Clint had been tortured by the thought of his growing need for Laurie, and by the realization that she, like Heather, would want far more from him than he could possibly give.

And now here she was, sitting on his sofa, waiting for him to sit down beside her. It was like a gift straight from heaven, and although Clint knew it could lead to trouble, he couldn't refuse it. The whole night had had a dreamlike quality anyway, and Laurie's invitation was just as otherworldly as the evening had already been. He lowered himself onto the sofa, feeling the reaction to his stress set into his bones. He felt an almost drugged warmth, even though his mind was perfectly alert.

There was barely a foot of space separating them, a scant twelve inches. It was filled with questions and buzzing with answers.

"You know, the common wisdom is that a hug can be a great reliever of stress," Laurie was saying, those great dark eyes of hers gleaming at him with what might have been suppressed fun and maybe something more.

"A hug, huh?"

"Yes." She waited a moment and then added, "For Heather, I mean. I was just thinking of ways to lighten things up between the two of you."

"Do you know anyone who could give me some pointers on how to go about it?" he said carefully, watching her eyes.

He was right. There *was* fun in them. He'd been right about the "something more," too.

"Well, I've had some training in stress reduction techniques," she said.

They were both aware that their bantering was just a delaying tactic, a shuffling for position while each tried to figure out what the other was feeling. Finally Laurie seemed certain or impatient—Clint couldn't tell which.

"First of all, you have to open your arms," she said. Her voice had been stable enough a minute ago. Now it was a husky whisper.

"Like this?"

"A little more. Good." She spread her own arms, inviting him in to the circle of her improbably virginal-looking nightgown. He was through with hesitation now. He shifted his weight on the sofa until he'd brought their bodies together, and the instant they touched, all traces of flippancy vanished from his mind. It was like sinking into a warm sea, like floating on the breeze. Like coming home.

He didn't stop to analyze his thoughts. He groaned as he moved against her, pulling them closer together, feeling her wrap her arms around his bare shoulders. The worn softness of the flannel felt good for the first two seconds, and then it seemed like a barrier. He wanted Laurie herself, the touch of her skin against his.

He heard his voice come out as a ragged moan. "I've never felt anything like being in your arms, Laurie."

His words made her move almost convulsively, twisting her body so that she lay half under him. He felt her curves fitting him in a way that first matched, then surpassed every erotic fantasy he'd had since he'd met her. He had been half-aroused when he'd turned from the fireplace to see her snuggled in the sofa; now, at the exquisite feel of her against the length of his body, there was no hiding from her how much he wanted her. Not in those flimsy pajama bottoms, at least.

Damn her clothes, anyway! Clint came close to suggesting that they do away with the whole shooting match, right down to her blue and green socks. Only the compelling need to taste her lips again kept him from saying it out loud.

Desire was boiling up in him like a hot spring. He wanted to claim her lips with every ounce of his strength, to pour everything he was feeling into his kiss. But something about the trusting way she tilted that small, pointed chin up to him made him slow down, and lower his mouth to hers with a gentleness that only banked the fires inside him.

It was the right thing to do. Her lips were soft and all-knowing, teaching him things he'd forgotten or had never really learned. At first the kiss was almost playful, each finding out how the other would react to a tentative nibble here or a gloss of the tongue there. Then, at last, it deepened and softened, and they let themselves be swept along into a place where the mutual pleasure of this sensual exploration was all that mattered.

Clint pulled her even closer to him, but it still wasn't enough. He needed to know how her skin would feel, if it could possibly be as smooth as he'd been dreaming it would be. He couldn't suppress a groan as he felt Laurie move against his thighs. The boldness of her hips against him destroyed what remained of his self-control.

He slid his left hand under the hem of her nightgown, past the waistband of her ragged jeans. The feel of her under his fingertips was electrifying, and he couldn't stop himself from moving on, inching higher until he encountered the welcoming roundness of her breast. It fit in his hand as though she'd been waiting for him all her life. The twin sensations of its center hardening against his palm and Laurie's moan vibrating against his mouth nearly drove him crazy.

New life was pouring through him, the longer he held her like this. He wanted to tell her how he felt, to ask her how she'd managed to lighten so many dark corners without even trying. But there were no words for what he was feeling, and he contented himself with kissing the smooth skin of her cheek, the long sweep of her neck, the throbbing hollow of her collarbone.

"I've never met anyone as giving as you," he whispered against her throat.

He sensed her smile. "I never met anyone I wanted to give to more," she replied. He tightened his arms around her, and then raised his head, looking down into passion-softened brown eyes that now seemed almost black.

"But Clint..." She was moving against him in a different way now, still exciting him, but making him wonder why her tone had changed subtly.

"What?" His voice was a lazy murmur. He bent to kiss her again, teasingly, and felt her breath quicken in response. But when she spoke again, there was a sense of purpose in her tone.

"I think our timing is way off."

Slowly, reality made its unwelcome way back into Clint's mind. "I guess we can't just pretend we're two teenagers getting carried away on the living-room sofa, can we?" he said ruefully. He raised himself slightly, not willing yet to let her go.

Something in her answering grin suggested she was struggling as hard against passion as he was. "I don't know about you," she said, "but I could do without pretending I'm a teenager, under any circumstances."

The second the words were out, Laurie clamped her lips shut in a vain effort to call them back. Of all the things to say to Clint....

The effect was just what she should have predicted. She saw the wariness come back into his eyes, and she could guess what he was thinking. "God, no," he said firmly. "Once was more than enough."

Well, she'd wanted to slow things down; she'd wanted to keep them both from getting carried away at the wrong time and in the wrong place. They should be paying attention to Heather tonight, not to their growing need for each other. But she hadn't meant to bring them back to reality so brutally, to catapult Clint back into his private world of bad memories.

Hoping to soften the blow, she reached up a hand and ran it through his hair. It fell against her fingers like a handful of heavy satin.

He looked startled by the gesture, the way he had the first time she'd touched him. Damn, she thought miserably. They were going to have to get things out in the open soon. She couldn't stand being so drawn to him, and yet so shut out of what he was feeling inside.

"Should we check on Heather?" His voice was gruff as he pushed himself up to a sitting position.

"It's not a bad idea."

She watched him as he got off the sofa and headed for his bedroom to get the blood-sugar testing kit he kept there.

The stubborn reminder of his desire was still clear under those lightweight pajamas. In spite of all her common sense Laurie couldn't help imagining how it would feel to let Clint sweep her into that big master bedroom with him, and fill her heart and soul and body with his loving.

She sighed, and tried to push her hair into some kind of order. Sleep and Clint Daniels had made a real beehive out of it.

She was almost calm and collected again by the time he came out of the bedroom. He'd put on a pair of jeans, she noted, and a baggy sweatshirt, as if the clothing might be some protection against the naked desire she'd felt when he'd crushed her against his strong chest. There were so many complex layers to this man, she thought, and at the moment she felt as though she'd barely scratched the surface.

Heather's blood sugar had returned to a more normal level, Laurie was glad to discover. She explained to Clint what to do if the level dropped again in two or three hours. "The glucagon in the fridge should take care of it, if that happens," she said. "Do you want me to stay, and relieve you? You can get a little sleep that way."

More than once, she'd noticed him covering up a jaw-cracking yawn that a less determined man would have let loose. "What about you?" he asked. "You have to work tomorrow, don't you?"

"I hate to say it, but tomorrow is today already," she admitted, "but I'll stay if you want me to."

She made the offer sincerely, but also because she wanted to know whether Clint's attitude had changed enough to admit that he needed help. He was such a proud, self-reliant man, but the strain of caring for his daughter by himself was obviously beginning to wear him down. She knew, better than most, how difficult that lonely sense of responsibility could be.

He stood there considering her offer for a long minute, and then he said, "You know, I think I *would* feel better if you were here for a while longer. Just to make sure I'm interpreting the blood-sugar readings correctly."

The relief that flooded through her made her smile at him. "I'd be glad to," she said. She saw in his watchful blue eyes that he wasn't completely happy with himself for asking her to stay and she was careful not to press the point. He'd asked—that was enough for now.

She bit down on a yawn herself, noticing that Heather's bedside clock radio was announcing the obscene hour of four-fifteen in the morning. She still felt keyed-up, energized first by the emergency and then by the incredible flood of sensation Clint's closeness on the sofa had triggered. But she could tell that the big man in front of her was almost dead on his feet.

"Go and get some sleep," she urged, giving him a gentle shove toward the door. "I'll call you when there's something for you to do."

"Sleep." He repeated the word slowly, as if he wasn't sure what she meant. "Sleep seems like a good idea."

He let her steer him out the door, and then paused. "You don't know how good this feels," he said.

"I can guess," Laurie replied. Only his strong will was keeping that muscular body upright, she thought. The sudden look of exhaustion in his eyes tugged at her heart. It was as if the simple act of asking for help had crystallized for him just how tired he was of coping on his own. "Go. Sleep."

He responded to the one-syllable orders with a faint smile and headed for his bedroom. Laurie watched him until he disappeared into the bedroom, and sighed. The old sweatshirt did nothing to hide the athletic breadth of his back, and even when he was dog-tired his masculine strength couldn't help but catch her eye. Maybe someday, she

thought, watching his door half close and picturing herself
on the other side of it with him.

Now that he was out of range, she found her professional habits coming back more reliably. She'd cultivated
the habit of catnapping during those long nights as an
emergency room nurse, and she found she could still grab
a quick doze now, and wake automatically to test Heather's blood sugar at six o'clock. By then, the girl was stirring, asking what had happened.

"You had a bad insulin reaction," Laurie said, "but
you're okay now. Try to go back to sleep."

"Do I have to go to school tomorrow?" Heather asked
groggily. "I feel so tired."

"I think it would be better if you stayed home," Laurie
said.

"Good." Heather's brown eyes, so unlike her father's
piercing blue ones, were drifting closed already. "I got a
part in a play, Laurie."

"That's great, Heather. Did you tell your dad?"

"Yeah."

"What did he say?"

Laurie was holding the girl's hand, trying to lull her back
to sleep. But a part of her genuinely wanted to know what
Clint's reaction had been.

"He said, 'That's good.'" Heather snuggled over onto
her side, comfortable with Laurie's presence. "That's all he
ever says." Her voice was growing sleepier. "No, sometimes he says 'That's bad.' But it's all just words. He
doesn't *feel* anything about any of it."

Laurie had to work hard to keep her hand from tightening around Heather's. She didn't want to disturb the al-
most-sleeping girl with her own sudden thoughts. Like hell
he doesn't feel anything, she wanted to say. As she sat in
Heather's bedroom watching the light outside grow slowly

stronger, she racked her brains and wished again that she could remember the ending to the story of the king who had turned his daughter into gold.

Six

"Fun date I turned out to be, didn't I?"

Laurie smiled at the familiar deep voice on the telephone. It was noon, and she'd been on the point of going out for lunch when Nelson had stuck his head in the door to ask if she wanted to talk to Clinton Daniels.

"Most fun I've had at an insulin reaction in a long time," she replied, sitting back down in her chair. She could picture the hidden smile, deep down in those startlingly blue eyes, that went with his bantering tone.

"I can't believe you're still awake. How do you do it?"

"Years of training. Believe me, I'll crash when I go home tonight. I'll probably be asleep by eight."

"Well, since you're probably not up for a wild evening of fun, how about coming over and having lunch with me and Heather? We're just surfacing now, believe it or not."

Laurie believed it. When she'd left that morning at eight to go home to shower and change, both Clint and his daughter had still been sleeping heavily. She'd been unable to resist the temptation to look into Clint's big bedroom, and had found herself unexpectedly moved and attracted by the sight of him. Sleep made him look younger somehow. The tension in him had dissolved, and he'd wished she had the courage to move closer to him and push back that thick tawny hair where it had fallen across his sleeping face. She'd felt oddly like Sleeping Beauty, getting a chance to turn the tables on the handsome prince.

"It doesn't surprise me that you slept in," she said. "You and Heather both had a lot to recover from. I'd love to have lunch with you. How's Heather doing?"

There was a pause, and then an uncharacteristic short laugh. "Better," he said cryptically. And that seemed to be all he was prepared to say on the subject. Intrigued, Laurie finished the conversation and hung up the phone, wondering what was going on in his mind now.

She got part of the answer as soon as Clint answered her knock on the door. He was wearing his jeans and that navy sweatshirt again, and he still had some of that younger, more appealing look to him that she'd been so drawn to earlier this morning. It was as if he'd unclenched himself a little.

Laurie wondered if the unclenching had anything to do with the fact that it was Heather—wearing an apron and stirring a pot of soup—who stood over the stove.

"I see you have a new chef," Laurie said, as Clint hung up her winter coat.

"He said I could make whatever I wanted for lunch." Heather sounded even more surprised than Laurie was. "I hope you like tomato soup, Laurie."

"I love it. That couldn't have come out of a can. It smells too good."

"It came out of that last cookbook you gave us." Clint came back into the kitchen, and started getting bowls and cutlery out of the cupboards. "And as to why we have a new chef, I felt so beat this morning that I decided I'd share some of the cooking around here for a change.''

His tone was light, but Laurie wasn't fooled by his words. Neither was Heather, judging by her quick smile. Clint might be pretending he was spreading the workload around, but they all knew this change in routine meant something far different. For the first time he was loosening his iron control over his daughter's life, letting her share in decisions that until now, he'd kept firmly in his own hands.

Lunch was delicious. Clint remembered some muffins he'd made and frozen a week ago, and popped them into the microwave oven.

"It smells like baking day at Grandma's," Laurie said, breathing deeply. "I may never want to go back to grabbing a quick sandwich at lunchtime again."

"You mean nutritionists don't practice what they preach, and sit down to a well-balanced meal three times a day?" Clint teased.

"Not nutritionists with a living to make," she replied. "You see, I have these people coming to my door at all hours of the day—"

"And night," Clint put in.

"Good point. And some days I'm lucky if I *can* grab a sandwich, let alone a well-balanced meal."

"What time do you have to be back today?" Clint asked.

Laurie looked at her watch. "My first appointment this afternoon called to reschedule, so I don't have to be back until two," she said.

"Good." Clint didn't elaborate. The three of them chatted easily for the rest of the meal, and carried the dishes over to the dishwasher when they were done.

"You just made a grave tactical error, honey," Clint said, as he rinsed his soup bowl. Heather looked up at him, startled, but Clint was smiling as he spoke. "That soup was so good, you may have just walked into a permanent job as cook.''

"Does that mean I don't have to spend so much time on my homework?" In spite of her light words, Heather was obviously thrilled by her father's praise.

"Good try, honey. And speaking of homework, don't you have a history essay to finish?"

Heather groaned. "I'll do it later," she said. "I'm still kind of tired. I thought I'd take a nap first, okay?"

Laurie found herself holding her breath, waiting to see whether Clint would treat this as a serious suggestion, or just another teenage ploy for avoiding something Heather didn't want to do. The girl *did* look tired; her skin was still pale and there were pronounced circles under her eyes.

She could see Clint wanting to lay down the law, as he was used to doing, but at the very last second he glanced at Laurie and seemed to change his mind. "A nap isn't a bad idea," he said slowly. "Just make sure the essay gets done eventually, all right?"

Heather smiled at him, and then, apparently on a sudden impulse, stood on tiptoe to kiss him on the cheek. It was impossible to say which of the three of them was more startled by the spontaneous gesture.

When the girl was gone, Clint let out a long breath. He looked tired, too, but there was something new in his expression that Laurie liked very much, something that made him more approachable than he'd ever been before.

He spoke quickly, as if he didn't want to give her time to comment on the change in his relationship with his daughter. "The reason I asked what time you had to go back to work is that I thought you might like to take a quick swim first," he said.

The immediate image of Clint in his minimalist swimming trunks pushed its way into Laurie's mind. "I don't have a suit with me," she protested.

"I knew you'd say that. That's why I ran out this morning and bought you one."

She couldn't help laughing at his smugness. "How do you know you got the right size?" she demanded.

The burning intensity of his gaze stopped her laughter short. There was open desire in the way he was looking at her, and his words underscored the expression in his eyes. "All I had to do was remember how you felt in my arms," he said. "I don't think I was far wrong about the size." His voice was a little hoarse, as if he was speaking past the same sudden ache that she felt in her own throat.

"So what do you say?" he asked. "Do you have time for a swim?"

"Are you kidding? When I think of how toasty and warm that heated floor was, how can I say no?" She was trying to speak lightly, and not quite succeeding. Her imagination was racing, picturing their two bodies meeting under the water's caress, as slick and urgent as spawning salmon.

A few minutes later, when she emerged from the changing room in a bathing suit that fit her like a glove, Clint had a hard time reminding himself that he'd intended this invitation as a pleasant interlude, not a prelude to seduction. But at the sight of her fit, curvaceous body in the deep aquamarine suit, and the way that plunging neckline drew his eye irresistibly to the hollow between her breasts, he wondered how he was going to keep himself from carrying her off bodily there and then.

She slipped into the pool as he watched, and he wondered if she, too, was aware of how charged the atmosphere was between them. He certainly wasn't keeping any secrets: he'd never really considered the disadvantages of tight red trunks in the company of a woman who excited him as much as Laurie Houston did. He followed her into the pool, letting the water hide his growing arousal. He was lost in memories of how her skin had felt against his palm, and the rush of feeling her responses had evoked in him.

"It's a perfect fit, Clint," she said, and it took a moment for him to realize she was talking about the suit. "I think I'll let you buy all my bathing suits from now on."

She shot him that stunning smile, and Clint felt suddenly dizzy, light-headed. He pushed himself off the side of the long, narrow pool and swam lazily toward her. "I have lots of talents you probably haven't suspected yet," he said, and saw her eyes widen as she took in his intended meaning.

"I'm sure you do," she murmured. She let herself float in the heated water, keeping just out of reach. "And I just discovered another one today."

"What's that?"

His mind was only half on their conversation. Something about the easy way she moved under the water was hypnotizing him, washing over his senses with an erotic persuasion he hadn't anticipated. His need for Laurie was pounding through him like waves on a hard sand beach.

"I mean the way you were with Heather. I'm so glad to know that things can be different between you two. You just disproved the adage about not being able to teach an old dog new tricks."

"Are you calling me an old dog?"

"I'm serious, Clint. I'm sure you're going to find life will be a lot easier if the two of you can be partners, instead of adversaries."

For a moment, he *was* serious. "I thought I was going to lose her last night," he said bluntly, stopping his progress by putting a hand on the side of the pool. "That changed the way I was thinking about things, I guess." The admission put a damper on the way he'd been letting himself be carried away by the growing desire he was feeling for this woman.

"I can understand that. And I'm glad to see it."

She was swimming slowly toward him now, using a sort of breaststroke that kept her dark head above the water. She'd pinned her hair up, and it accented her slender neck and pointed, determined chin.

With an effort that was nearly physical in the amount of willpower it took, Clint made himself pause and consider what was going on here. He'd meant what he'd said to Laurie: his attitude toward his daughter had changed, and he hoped it was for the better. He hated to give up the control he'd always insisted upon, but the thought of the way Heather had kissed him with such open affection was worth it.

That *didn't* mean everything in his life was going to change, though. Changing things with his daughter didn't erase all the unresolved feelings he was still grappling with. Love, for Clint, had always been a two-edged sword. And somehow, in letting Laurie Houston get this close to him, he felt he was perilously close to cutting himself on that particular blade again.

"How far do you usually swim?" she was asking, recalling him to the present.

"At least a half mile. Less, when Heather and I work out together."

"Doesn't she like to swim?"

"She's not wild about it."

"That's hard to imagine. I'd kill to have a pool like this in my own home."

Laurie had seen the shadow cross Clint's face, and she'd moved closer to him, hoping to erase it. But she'd forgotten how tricky it was to maneuver under water. She'd meant to stop a couple of feet from him, but she hadn't planned it soon enough. Without meaning to, she glided right into him, and heard him inhale suddenly as he gathered her to him. It was like being cradled by a water god, she thought hazily.

"I might not have suggested a swim at all, if I'd known it was going to excite your murderous tendencies," he said.

"Speaking of excited tendencies..." She couldn't resist it. The way his nearly naked body made her feel was too insanely seductive. She let the gentle motion of the water rock her hips against his, and felt his need for her growing as the wavelike rhythm created an erotic caress.

"It's going to take us a long time to get to a half mile at this rate," she said. An expectedly strong wave pushed her more intimately against him, and she gasped as the very core of her body responded to the movement. "It feels like the pool's got other ideas for us, doesn't it?"

"I don't think we can blame the pool." Clint's voice was as husky as hers. He sounded as though he was struggling against a hunger that would not be contained. "After all, we made the waves, didn't we?"

Laurie lifted her eyes to his and saw that their brilliant blue was nearly eclipsed by the darkness of desire. She wondered if her own eyes were as dark, and whether that accounted for the sudden tightening of Clint's grip as he looked down at her.

"You're not safe, woman," he growled. For a long moment she thought he was going to kiss her, and she found herself aching for his kiss. But he was still holding himself back, and suddenly she needed to know why.

"Clint?" Her voice sounded uncertain. "You seem angry about something. Are you?"

"Angry? No."

He held her against the wet strength of his chest a moment longer, as if to prove his words, and then he let her go, and swam off slowly. She followed him with her eyes, trying to steady her breathing.

"Then what's wrong?"

She could see the struggle in his face. "I don't know what we're getting into here, Laurie. I don't know where it might lead."

"Do you have to know? Can't we just follow along, and see what happens?"

"No." The blunt syllable didn't leave any room for compromise. "That's not how I do things. It's not how I've ever done them."

She thought of his careful research into the businesses he took over, and the way he'd built up his fortune. Was all of that an attempt to overcome the painful uncertainty of his early years?

"You can't force a relationship to be just the way you want it," she said cautiously. "I think you've already seen that with Heather."

"This has nothing to do with Heather. I'm talking about you and me."

"I know you are. And I'm saying—"

He overrode her words. "*I'm* saying there's something between us. It's impossible to ignore. I'm just not sure where to go with it next."

She could feel him fighting his own desires. It was a contest between his own memories of his poisoned past and the hope for a new life that she saw in his eyes whenever she was close to him. And suddenly Laurie knew she had to take a stand for that fledgling hope. Recklessly, she pushed off the side of the pool and approached him again. This time, she did manage to stop just short of touching him, but the water between them felt superheated, as though their slippery bodies had been jolted into contact anyway.

"You want to know what I think, Clint?" She didn't wait for his answer. "I think you've been pushing yourself too hard for too long. I think you've lost your sense of perspective."

"What do you mean?" he asked.

"You obviously live by a set of rules you've made for yourself. But maybe they need to change a little."

She could see she was on tricky ground here. "Any rules I live by, I learned the hard way," he said.

"What *are* those rules?" she asked him, letting the water move them a little closer.

He cleared his throat. "Not to jump into things before I know all the angles," he said. "Not to lose control of things any more than I have to. Not to—"

He hesitated over that one. Laurie thought she knew what he was about to say. "Not to trust anyone to get too close?" she supplied.

She didn't like the shuttered look that came into his eyes at that. "Something like that," he admitted.

"Not even when you feel...like this?" The swaying movement of the water brought them against each other again, and Laurie knew his whole frame was singing with the same longing that filled her. Clint closed his eyes, still trying to fight his desire, and then let out a long breath as he closed his arms around her.

"You make a good case, Ms. Houston," he breathed against her hair. Laurie was reveling in their nearness, the feelings of desire and comfort that seemed combined in equal parts. She hadn't known, until just now, how much she wanted to give in to both.

"Clint," she whispered, "why is it we always seem to saddle ourselves with a chaperon?"

He flickered a glance at the closed door of Heather's room, and smiled grimly. "Good point," he said. "Laurie, if I hold you like this for one minute more, I can't be responsible for what happens, chaperon or no chaperon."

"Just one more minute." She couldn't bear to move away so soon, not when he'd just relaxed against her like a magnificent marble statue come to life.

She felt him pull her even closer, felt her breasts crushed against him and her hips meeting his in an intimate preview that left her gasping. His fingers trickled across her bare back and against her neck like rivulets of warm water, and every move he made increased the hunger inside her.

She was losing herself in pure sensation when she heard him mutter against her hair, "I have to fly to Toronto this weekend for a quick business meeting. I was going to ask you if you could stay here with Heather, but if I can find someone else to keep an eye on her, will you come with me?"

A warning bell went off in the far outer reaches of her mind. She didn't like the thought that he'd been planning to recruit her as a temporary parent for Heather. But for the moment, the alluring feel of his skin against hers, and the heady thought of what a weekend together would bring, were enough to keep her misgivings well below the surface.

She raised her eyes to his, and knew that the look on her face would give him her answer even before she whispered, "Yes."

Laurie had never been in a plane like this one. She'd flown coast to coast several times on big planes, and many times from Timmins to Toronto or Montreal on smaller commercial crafts. But none of those had had cabins that looked like living rooms, as this one did. None had featured comfortable seats that were more like easy chairs, or an interior design scheme that made her wonder if all privately chartered jets were this tastefully decorated.

Most important of all, none of the planes she'd boarded before had had Clint on them.

He'd met her at the Timmins airport, and taken her small suitcase with an impersonal gallantry that left her wondering what was going on in his mind today. He was dressed for the business meeting he'd told her about, in his navy pinstriped suit and a brilliantly white shirt. Only the bold red of his tie hinted that he was anything beyond just another businessman on the way to a conference. Something about the tie, and the suppressed feelings she saw in his eyes, warned Laurie that his mood was more volatile since their sensuous encounter in the pool earlier this week.

"How long is your meeting likely to last?" she asked him, as they sat down opposite each other in the cabin and buckled their seat belts.

"Two hours, maybe three." The fact that he wasn't looking into her eyes made her a little uneasy.

"Then I may go out and do some shopping," Laurie said, trying to speak casually. "Do you have anywhere specific in mind for dinner?"

It was like trying to draw out an uncommunicative stranger. The more questions Laurie asked, the shorter Clint's answers became, until somewhere over central Ontario, she lost patience with him and asked the direct question that had been on her mind since she'd met him at the airport.

"Clint, are you having second thoughts about this?"

That got a reaction out of him. He'd been looking silently out the window, but now his head spun around. "What makes you say that?" he demanded.

"Just that you're not very good at hiding your moods, that's all."

One corner of his mouth lifted in a smile that wasn't amused at all. "And here I thought I was being so cool," he said.

"We don't have to pursue this, you know. I can catch a flight back to Timmins, and leave you to your business in Toronto." The idea made her voice wobble; she hadn't realized until just that moment how much she was looking forward to spending this weekend with Clint.

"Don't even think about it." His immediate response reassured her, as did the way he leaned forward to take her hands in his. The physical contact reminded her again of how strong the attraction between them was, although today his hands, uncharacteristically, were as cold as hers usually were. As cold as those blue eyes, she thought anxiously.

"Then what's wrong, Clint? I need to know."

"I know you do." He sighed, sounding almost angry. "I wouldn't say I'm having second thoughts. But I guess I still haven't sorted through what my *first* thoughts are."

She made herself keep silent, waiting for him to go on. He was moving his thumb over her palm as he spoke, in slow circles that couldn't help but remind her of the way his hands had felt on her bare skin. There was an almost magnetic current in his touch, connected to the source of every pleasurable sensation in her body.

Finally he looked at her. She could see the confusion in his eyes. "I just never anticipated this," he said. "It's not part of what I had envisioned for my life. I don't—" He hesitated, and then went on. "I'm not very good at sharing myself, Laurie, as you've already pointed out. I'm learning to do it with Heather, because I can see that it makes her situation a lot easier."

Laurie's heart went out to him. He was like a child trying to learn something he didn't fully understand yet, she thought.

"Is that the only reason you're trying to change the situation with Heather?" she asked. "Isn't it because you love her, too?"

His reply seemed forced out of him. "I don't think I understand what people mean when they talk about love," he said. "Other people always seem to see love as a good thing, pure and simple. My experience has been that it can be a curse as well as a blessing."

Not for the first time, Laurie's heart ached for the lonely, frightened boyhood Clint must have had. "So you can't trust what's happening between us," she said slowly.

His blue eyes begged her to understand. "It simply doesn't fit in with the way I'm used to living my life," he said.

That irritated her. "Clint, I have to admit I'm getting a little tired of stepping around all these rules of yours," she said. "Do you have to fit everything that happens to you into some preconceived plan?"

"Yes," he replied harshly. "That's how I've survived, how I've made things happen on my terms."

"There are other ways of surviving, you know," she said softly. "And sometimes you can't make things happen just the way you want them to. You can't always be the one in control. Life just isn't like that."

"Don't patronize me, Laurie." There was real annoyance in his voice now, though she couldn't tell which of them it was aimed at. "I know life's not like that. It's uncertain, and sometimes damned dangerous. And that's why you need some defenses to deal with it."

"Defenses against people who are close to you?" She'd wanted to say *people you love, people who love you*. But she'd already figured out that the very word *love* would trigger all kinds of buried and painful emotions in him.

"Sometimes those most of all." His voice was definitely angry now, warning her to drop the subject. But Laurie couldn't do that. She was aching for Clint, wishing she could somehow heal the old wounds that had built up this barrier of scar tissue around his heart.

"I don't want you to think I'm condemning you," she said, leaning a little closer to him. "I know what a hard time you had when you were younger. I can understand how being treated the way you were could sour anybody on love and trust."

She'd spent so much time thinking about Clint's history, agonizing over the story she'd read in the paper, that the words were out before she realized she hadn't told him yet how much of his story she knew. And from the sudden sharp drawing in of his breath, and the darkening of his eyes, she had a feeling she could have spoken the news to him more carefully.

"And is that supposed to mean?" His tone wasn't friendly at all.

She could feel him tugging his hands away, but she pulled against him, trying to force him to stay. "Just that I know about what happened to you when you were sixteen," she said. "Clint, just listen to me."

Fat chance. She could read the refusal in his eyes even before he freed himself from her fingers. With one impatient motion he unfastened his seat belt and stood up. At full height, inside the private jet, he looked more muscular and imposing than ever. His broad shoulders in that dark blue suit seemed to fill the space around him.

"Talk about trust!" he said scornfully. "How long have you been sneaking around researching me?"

"Sneaking around!" Laurie repeated the words, stung. "If it makes any difference, I found out most of your story by accident. George MacDonald grew up in Timmins, as he probably told you. When he first met you, he thought you seemed familiar, and shortly after he referred you and Heather to me, he remembered who you were. He came and told me what he knew."

"And what did he know?" His heavy tone warned her to be cautious.

"That your real name is Daniel Lindstrom."

"My real name is Clinton Daniels. I had it legally changed."

"All right, then. Your name *used* to be Daniel Lindstrom."

He dragged a hand across his eyes. With the sudden tiredness that came across his face, he seemed older again, the way he'd looked when they'd first met.

"And you grew up in Timmins."

"What else?" He wasn't volunteering any information of his own, she noticed. She felt exactly the way she had when quaking her way through oral exams at nurse's college.

"Your father was...well, I believe George called him 'a tough case.'"

"Tactful of him. My father was a violent alcoholic."

Laurie shuddered at the bleak sound in his voice. "And when you were sixteen, he beat you so badly you ended up in intensive care. After that experience you left Timmins."

"Anything else?"

She drew in a deep breath. "I don't know, Clint. Maybe you'd care to add a few details. It's your story, after all."

He'd started pacing up and down in the limited space of the cabin, like a caged lion again. Now he rounded on her, so suddenly that she had a momentary fear the balance of the small plane would be upset.

"No," he said tightly. "That was Daniel Lindstrom's story. I left him behind when I was sixteen, remember?"

"But you're still carrying around all the things that happened to him. And that's spilling over into what's happening between us. Can't you see that?"

At least he'd stopped pacing. But his stillness was almost menacing, and she couldn't help wondering which way he would spring next.

"Of course I can see it," he said finally. "What I'm telling you is that there's nothing I can do about it. And believe me, I've tried."

Laurie drew in a shaky breath. "Maybe I'd understand better if you gave me your version of just what did happen," she said boldly.

"It's not very pleasant," he warned her.

"I'm not looking for a bedtime story, Clint. I just want to know how you feel."

He gave a short laugh, sounding surprised at himself. "You know, in the past twenty years I've never talked about this with anyone," he said.

Laurie could believe that. The very first time she'd seen him, she'd read in his eyes the effort it took to suppress all those twenty-year-old bad feelings.

"Want to tell me about it?" she asked. She was trying to sound casual, interested but not pushy.

He paced to the end of the cabin, then back again. Suddenly, as if his mind was made up, he flung himself back into his seat and glared at her, long legs stretched out in front of him. "I'll give you the bare bones," he said. "Anything else makes me feel like punching the walls."

Well, it was a start. Laurie nodded, and said, "Punching the walls in here doesn't seem like such a great idea. Just tell me what you want to."

He leaned his head back against the seat rest, and studied the ceiling. "You have to imagine the kind of place I lived in," he said. "It wasn't much more than a shack."

Laurie didn't have to imagine it. She'd seen some of the outlying areas around Timmins, and they were just as rough as George had told her they were.

"Then you have to imagine a man with a lot of ability, but no education and no opportunities. A man surrounded by other men who drank to escape the fact that they were stuck out in the bush with no hope of anything better coming along any time soon. That was my father."

He'd said he didn't want to go beyond the bare bones, but Laurie couldn't help asking, "Did you love him?"

He transferred his glare from the ceiling to her, and she almost wished she'd stayed silent. "Yes," he said roughly. "The hell of it was, I *did* love him. He was all the family I had. And nine days out of ten he could make me feel like a million bucks—like I could succeed at anything I tried. On the tenth day, he'd beat the hide off me."

"Clint . . . why?"

"I never knew. One day he'd treat me as though I was his pride and joy—taking me fishing, letting me drive his old truck, talking about all the great things I could do with my life. And the next day, *wham!* I couldn't string two words together without his coming down on me like a sledgehammer."

"And you still loved him." Laurie's words were soft, more for her own ears than Clint's.

He heard them anyway. "Yes," he said, just as softly, but with a tension like a tightly strung wire in his voice. "I still loved him. And that's how I learned that love isn't a simple emotion, Laurie. There can be fear in it, too. Or anger. And it made me see that the best way to survive is to learn to depend on no one but yourself."

"But Clint..." Laurie leaned forward, wishing she could reach him somehow. His big hands were clenched over the arms of his seat, and she had a feeling that prying them off would take more muscle than she had. "I haven't treated you that way. I haven't given you any reason *not* to trust me, have I?"

His eyes were narrowed now, assessing her. "Not yet," he said. "But that doesn't mean you never would. I'm sorry." His apology had a desperate sound to it, as though he hated hearing his own words. "That's what I meant when I said I couldn't see where this relationship would lead, Laurie. I've never gotten into the habit of trusting people. Hell, maybe I can't trust anyone—I don't know for sure. But it's too soon to start making predictions about our future. I want you to know that, before we go any further."

She was silent then, wondering what it would take to win his trust. At least he'd opened up to her this much. That had to be a good sign.

On the other hand, it seemed that calling up his unhappy memories had done nothing to improve his mood. He was drumming his fingertips restlessly against the arm of his chair and looking away from her again, out the window.

The tight feeling in her ears told Laurie the plane was starting to make its descent, and out her own window she could see the increasingly larger towns to the north of Toronto, so different from the miles of wilderness around Timmins.

"I'm still willing to go on, if you are," she said suddenly. It was important to let him know that she cared about him enough to take a chance on their future together. The word *love* flashed through her mind again. Was she in love with Clint Daniels? As he turned those haunted, startlingly blue eyes on her again, she began to think that she was.

"You're either a very brave woman," he said, with a touch of grudging relief in his tone, "or a crazy one."

Laurie let out her breath. "Maybe a bit of both," she said, and swallowed hard to clear more than just her ears.

Seven

The hotel was in the heart of downtown Toronto, and their eleventh-floor room looked out on Lake Ontario and the island parks on the far side of Toronto Harbour. Laurie was enjoying the view on her own, because Clint had stayed in the taxi that had brought them from the airport, and gone straight to his business meeting.

"If you go out shopping, be sure you're back in time for dinner," he'd warned her, as the bellhop loaded their suitcases onto a trolley. "There's a Greek place over on Danforth Avenue that you're going to love."

"I'll be here," Laurie promised. She knew already that she wanted to be waiting when Clint got back. She was feeling closer to him all the time, and even his taciturn mood at the end of their flight had only made her want to pursue this attraction further.

By four o'clock, when he still wasn't back, Laurie decided to treat herself to a long soak in the tub. The hotel room was warm, but her chronically chilly toes hadn't quite received the message yet. Maybe some hot water would help.

She ran the tub as full as she could, and poured in the bubble bath the hotel had provided. Then she pinned up her hair and slid into the sweetly scented bath, feeling her toes sting as she eased them into the steaming water. She'd only been soaking for a few minutes—just long enough for her feet to start to warm up—when she heard the door to the hotel room open. She kept very still, listening.

She knew it was Clint. From the beginning she'd had an aching, physical awareness when he was in a room with her. Her heart started to beat a little faster, just picturing him.

She heard him set down his briefcase, and then make a quick tour of the room. "Damn," he said softly. She realized he must have thought she was out somewhere.

"Damn, nothing," she called, sitting up in the tub. "I'm in here."

He was wearing his sheepskin coat, spotted with the late-winter snow that was falling outside. His imposing physique was overpowering in the small bathroom. Laurie looked up at him and grinned, watching him shred the coat and the suit jacket under it.

"Did you think I'd run out on you?" she asked.

He didn't seem relaxed enough to share her grin. "I thought you might have found shopping more appealing than my company," he said.

She shook her head at him, and felt the hot water moving around her body. There was something warm and liquid inside of her, too, and it was beginning to suffuse her as Clint kneeled by the tub and loosened his tie.

"I guess it's a little hot in here," she said.

"It's fine." He seemed impatient with small talk, as well as with his clothing. He tossed the tie over the back of the toilet, and unbuttoned his shirt cuffs as he spoke.

"Laurie, I owe you several apologies," he said.

"You do?"

"Yes. I was pretty insufferable earlier today. I'm amazed that you put up with it."

She sat up a little straighter. There were bubbles clinging to her upper body, but Clint's proximity made her feel naked and desirable.

"I wouldn't call your behavior insufferable—" she began, but he stopped her.

"Insufferable is putting it kindly," he said. Cuffs unbuttoned, he started on his collar buttons. She felt half-hypnotized by the sight of the curling dark blond hair on his chest as his fingers deftly flicked the shirt buttons open.

"I can understand why talking about your past is hard for you," she said. "You have every right to find it difficult."

"But I don't have a right to saddle you with everything that happened to me in the past," he said.

Clint was finding it harder and harder to talk. The moment he'd stepped into the bathroom and breathed in the warm, scented air, it had been nearly impossible for him to think clearly. The sight of Laurie's dark head and flashing eyes, and her barely hidden curves floating in those clouds of white bubbles, had started a fever in his blood that was rapidly taking over all his rational thought processes. He wanted to apologize to her for his having been such a bear this morning; and then he wanted all words to be over and done with.

For perhaps the first time in his life, Clint Daniels, man of infinite caution and ironclad rules about never rushing into something new and unknown, wanted to plunge himself, body and soul, into the woman he was kneeling beside. He wanted to forget the past and ignore the future. And Laurie seemed to hold the magical key that would let him do that, somewhere in the depths of her luminous brown eyes.

"I don't know how to say this, Laurie," he said raggedly, stripping off his white shirt. It joined his tie on the back of the toilet. The heated air felt good on his bare torso as he leaned closer to the edge of the tub. "I want this weekend to be just for the two of us, alone, without thinking of what went before or what might come after. Can we do that?"

There was a momentary shadow on her face, as if she wasn't sure. Then, as he reached out a hand that trembled slightly, and scooped up a warm handful of water very close to her breasts, she gave him the ghost of a smile, and said softly, "Are you sure you're the same man who says he has to plan and investigate every single move he makes?"

"No," he said bluntly. "I'm not sure I'm the same man. At the moment I'm not sure of anything, except how much I want you."

He heard her sudden gasp, as he emptied his hand and trailed it along the surface of the water until he met the slickness of her skin. Both of them groaned at the intimate contact, and Clint saw Laurie's eyes half close.

"Laurie," he said urgently, "I've never met anyone in my life who could make me feel like this."

Her eyes opened again, languidly, and he saw in them how supremely seductive a woman could be. He wanted to bring every exquisite part of her to the pinnacle of pleasure, to replace that lazy, sensuous smile with the astonishment of passion.

He could feel her breathing quicken under his hands, as he slowly caressed her breasts under the soap bubbles. Everything about her was soft and yielding—everything but the hard jewel of her nipple, like a diamond floating on a cloud of silk. He passed his thumb across its tightened peak, and felt his own response like a depth charge in his loins.

"Think we'd drown if I got in there with you?" he asked huskily.

She gave him a quick smile. "Maybe not," she said, "but we *would* overflow the tub, and probably cause a leak in the room downstairs."

"We don't want that." His hand was traveling slowly over her breasts, and Laurie's whole body arched involuntarily, following that lazy and tantalizing touch.

"No," she agreed breathlessly. "We don't want that. They'd probably send up some big hairy maintenance man to fix it—"

Her sentence ended on another gasp of pleasure. Clint was sliding his hand lower, across her stomach. She couldn't tell where the hot water left off and her body began. All of her was swimming with a warm haze of desire.

Clint chuckled softly. Was he responding to her words, or just pleased with what he was doing to her? "A big hairy maintenance man would kind of spoil the mood, wouldn't he?" he said.

"I'm . . . afraid so."

It was becoming impossible to speak. Her breath caught in her throat each time Clint discovered another part of her body that responded so generously to his caresses. She'd honestly never dreamed there were so many of them, or that a man's slightest touch could make her feel so completely abandoned.

She wanted to touch every inch of him, too. She wanted to feel their bodies intertwining, urging each other on. But she was trapped in the bathtub, a willing prisoner as long as Clint continued his erotic exploration.

His knowing fingers had already discovered the pulsating core of her, and the things he was doing to her were making her giddy. She could have sworn she was airborne, wafting along on a bed of soft white clouds. She let her head fall back, and felt him moving closer, letting his lips trail along the length of her throat and up to the base of her ear.

The sudden nearness of him was too much. She was about to tell him she couldn't stand much more of this, that she had to get out of the tub and into his arms before he drove her out of her mind. But before she could get the words out, his movements shifted slightly, and Laurie found herself being swept into a magical new place, where nothing mattered but the pleasure Clint was giving her.

She heard her voice, very far away, giving a startled cry. She rocked her hips against him, giving herself up to the primitive and pulsating rhythm inside her. And then, with a sudden convulsion, that rhythm shattered in a hundred different directions, and Laurie was overtaken by a sweet, mindless release.

When she finally opened her eyes, she found she had one arm tightly around Clint's shoulders, holding him as if she was afraid he would disappear. That knowing smile was still on his face, and she had a feeling she looked much the same.

"That smile of yours is going to drive me crazy someday," he was saying.

She had to speak around her own unsteady breathing. "We'll be even, then," she said. "Much more of this is going to drive *me* crazy."

His smile widened, making him look more than ever like a big benevolent cat. Laurie flicked her fingers across the surface of the water, spattering his broad chest with soap bubbles.

"Don't look so smug," she told him.

His reply was to hoist her to her feet and wrap her in one of the big white towels that was at hand. "That's not smugness," he informed her. "That, for your information, is a look of barely controlled frustration."

She widened her eyes, teasing him. "Is there anything *I* can do to help?" she asked.

She couldn't keep up the pretense of teasing. Her lids closed again in a sudden wave of renewed desire as her body met his. And his low growl was all the answer she wanted, anyway. The throbbing evidence of his need for her was more than enough to chase every other thought out of her mind.

He toweled her dry, roughly, thoroughly, and even that had an erotic double meaning that made Laurie's head spin. Suddenly she wanted to see all of him, to admire the lean curves of his muscles and the magnificently aroused maleness of him. She wanted to drink him in with all her senses, to taste the warm darkness of his mouth and breathe in the musky scent of his skin. She knew that haunting perfume was there, lurking beneath the sweet flowery bubble-bath scent that hung in the moist air.

She hauled in a long breath, her face pressed tightly against his strong shoulder. "You smell so good, Clint," she said.

His face was lost in her hair. Its thickness draped his features like a curtain shielding him from the rest of the world. "After-shave," he said unromantically, as he finished drying her off and wrapped her in the soft white towel.

She shook her head against him, and breathed in again. "Much better than that," she said. Her voice was muffled now. He had to bend a little lower to hear her.

His slight shift in position brought the heated centers of their bodies even closer together. Clint could feel her heart pounding, and guessed the degree of her desire for him in the way her breath came in unsteady gasps. He arched against her, knowing his own arousal could very easily explode into a burning immediacy if he let it.

He didn't want to let it. He'd waited too long for this moment. He had been waiting even before he'd met Laurie, he thought dimly. All his life he'd had an unacknowledged hope that someday, someone might open herself to him like this, invading him with the generous gift of her loving. He wasn't going to rush things now, even if his body was urging him on in no uncertain terms.

He led her into the bedroom, delighting in the way her graceful, athletic walk made her womanly curves seem even more luscious and desirable. Even half-hidden by the towel, she was more enticing than he'd dreamed.

"Your outfit gives new meaning to the phrase, 'the well-dressed businessman,'" she was saying, smiling again.

He followed her glance downward, and smiled himself. He'd only undressed as far as his waist; from the belt downward, he was still wearing his business clothes.

"That's easily taken care of," he said, letting go of her long enough to unbuckle his belt and shed his trousers and the rest of his clothes.

He pulled away the thick towel that was still draped around her. The sight of her was like a stab of exquisite pain, and he stepped closer, running both his hands over her full, rounded breasts and feeling their taut centers hard in the middle of his palms.

"Laurie..."

He wanted to tell her so many things, but he couldn't find the words. He had to show her, instead, prove to her that in this one way, at least, he was ready to open up to her in a way he'd never done with any other woman. With a deliberate slowness that he felt in every muscle of his thighs, he lowered himself in front of her, and stopped when his knees hit the soft carpet.

"It's impossible for anything to be this soft," he muttered, sliding his cheek into the hollow between her breasts. His lips found the curve of one, then the other.

Laurie felt a bolt of pleasure surge through her at the touch of his mouth against her cooling skin. His caress was warm, moist, infinitely patient and infinitely knowing. His tongue followed the round line of her breasts in a spiral that communicated dizzyingly to every nerve in her body. She heard her own astonished gasp as he finally reached the supersensitive nipples that had been tightly contracted ever since he'd first approached her in the tub.

His hands were smooth and supple, continuing to explore the outlines of her body. Laurie felt torn, wanting to enjoy every one of his caresses equally. His hands were heavenly, but his mouth... his mouth was magic.

Then, in one sudden motion that told her all over again just how much strength was hidden in those hard muscles of his, he pulled himself to his feet, dragging her against him. She felt herself being lifted from the floor, and held against the broad expanse of his chest. She loved the feel of her bare arm brushing over those tawny short curls that reminded her of the color of a lion's mane.

She felt the motion of his steps in every part of her. Their bodies seemed created to share each other's movements, she thought, and her mind raced ahead to the way they would feel sharing that most intimate motion of all.

He seemed determined to make her wait for that moment. He lowered her gently onto the bed, and she reached up and ran her hands over the taut muscles of his upper arms as he slowly released his grip.

"I never knew a man so strong could be so gentle," she said wonderingly.

Her words seemed to inflame him. She saw his jaw clench, and realized how tightly he was holding himself back, prolonging this pleasure.

"I want to be everything for you, Laurie," he said. His darkened eyes echoed the promise. "Strong and gentle, and much more. Lie back, and let me love you."

She sank back against the big bed, quivering mightily in places she'd barely suspected existed. He *was* everything, she thought: he was gentle, he was powerful, he was achingly vulnerable. She wrapped her arms tightly around his neck, silently trying to communicate to him how much she cared for him.

Her body clamored to feel him inside her, but still he was making her wait. Teasing her, he shifted himself to the very edge of the bed, and kissed her ankle. Laurie exhaled deeply, unsteadily. If he was this sensual and thorough with every part of her, she was sure she would vaporize into a mist of pure ecstasy before he got much above her knees.

He was just as thorough as she'd hoped and feared, kissing the inside of her calf, turning her lower leg in his hands as if he were a connoisseur admiring a priceless work of art that was suddenly his. The humming inside her peaked sharply when he suddenly shifted his caresses to her bare insole. She could feel the smooth persuasion of his lips, and the very slight roughness on his chin.

"Nobody ever kissed me there before," she whispered, half to herself.

She felt his lips curve against the unbearably sensual place. "Think what they were missing," he said. "I could feel your whole body shudder when I kissed that spot."

He proved his point by kissing her there again, then started a slow ascent that left Laurie helplessly longing for more. He revisited her ankle, the inside of her calf, the little hollow at the back of her knee—who could have known there were so many secret delights hidden in such an innocuous spot?—and still upward, moaning against the long smooth expanse of her upper thigh.

His hands ran ahead of him now. Laurie was barely aware of tangling her fingers in his thick sandy hair. All of her was focused on the places he was touching. He was setting off rockets in the inner recesses of her body, making her head swim with an almost dangerous lightness. She felt disconnected from the bed, from the hotel room, from everything but Clint's searching caresses and her own quivering response.

"Oh, Clint..."

He must have heard the urgency in her voice, because he abandoned that tantalizingly slow exploration of her body and lifted his head, pulling himself up to lie alongside her at the same time. His hand never stopped in its crazy enticement, as if he wanted to know how close to the edge he could drive her this time.

She had to tell him. "Clint, I want to feel you inside me," she said unevenly. "Please."

Clint felt a slow smile spread over his face. Laurie's body was one unending erogenous zone, and at the moment all he could think about was pushing their mutual pleasure to the very limits, filling her, body and soul. He lifted himself above her, feeling the passion in the dark pools of her eyes as a physical sensation. He'd never been this aroused, this sure, this kingly...

This unprepared. "Damn!" he muttered, and saw her eyes flicker uncertainly.

Reluctantly he moved to one side, reached for his pants and searched in one of the back pockets for the packet he'd armed himself with this afternoon. A thought flickered across his mind, like an unwelcome stray: this was still, after all, a momentary passion. He felt a tinge of his old reluctance when he thought of the possibility of anything more permanent.

The chilling thought passed when he looked back down at Laurie. She seemed unaware of his flash of misgiving, still begging him with those impossibly dark eyes to give her all the pleasure he'd promised. The instant he'd immersed himself in that brown-eyed appeal again, his sudden anxiety disappeared and he felt himself being swept back into the current of their passion.

She arched against him with a movement that made her desires crystal clear. He groaned, shifting himself slightly, and then in one long thrust he slid inside her. Every muscle in Laurie's body was clenched around him, holding him in the center of her and quivering with the magic of it.

They were almost perfectly still for a long drawn-out moment, neither of them willing to end that first searing revelation of just how perfectly they fit together. Laurie was aware of a throbbing pulse inside her, an invitation to Clint to move so slightly that at first it was nothing more than an intensifying of the sensation of having him fill her like this.

Then his movements became deeper, more definite, sliding gradually into an erotic rhythm that Laurie followed blindly. Every thrust seemed to awaken some new part of her, leaving her gasping his name out loud. Mindlessly she twined her legs around his, lost in the age-old drumbeat of pure passion, unable to think of anything but how right this felt.

He altered his balance point slightly, and she followed the subtle shift. It exposed a whole new world of pleasure, and Laurie felt herself sliding into it recklessly. They rocked together, deeper and still deeper yet, urging each other on to the moment they'd both known was there from the first time they'd touched—or was it a hundred years before then?

Laurie's arms were wrapped around Clint's neck, and suddenly she felt his tightly corded muscles harden even more. At the same instant, her own world changed, propelling her beyond rational thought to a new plane where all that mattered was this glorious moment. She was barely aware of Clint, of who she was, of what planet she was on, as the wave swept her up and carried her to its crest. She was poised there for one shattering second, and then in the next instant she dropped into an abyss of pleasure that left her shuddering and drained.

It took a moment to clear her thoughts, and to recall hearing Clint's hoarse cry at that same exquisite moment. His arms had tightened convulsively around her, and now, gradually, they began to loosen again. His breathing was labored, loud in the quiet room.

For a long time neither of them said anything. Finally Clint made an effort to calm his racing heartbeat, taking in a long breath and letting it out slowly. His voice still wasn't quite steady as he said, "For the first time since I met you, I think you're warm all the way through."

"'Warm' is one way to put it." Laurie looked up into his eyes, too shaken to manage a smile just yet. "'Astonished' is maybe more accurate."

"I am, too." He traced the outline of her face with a gentle forefinger. "At the risk of using a cliché, I didn't think it was possible to feel quite this way."

"Clichés are usually there for a good reason," she told him. She wondered, silently, if any lovers anywhere could possibly be as finely attuned to each other as she and Clint had just proven they were.

There was another long silence. It was finally broken by what sounded like distant thunder. Laurie frowned, then laughed. "Do I hear your stomach calling for food?" she said.

Clint chuckled. "It's mundane, but true. I've become so used to eating dinner early with Heather that the idea of eating fashionably late doesn't appeal to me anymore, I guess."

"I'm a little hungry myself," she admitted. "Are we going to that Greek place for dinner?"

"No," he said firmly. "That would mean going out in the cold and wet, and getting dressed, and getting out of this bed."

"But not necessarily in that order."

"Well, not quite. Anyway, I'm not prepared to do any of those things just at the moment. No, I think we'll let room service provide our dinner tonight, if that's all right with you."

In her present barely-connected-to-the-earth mood, Laurie was happy to go along with whatever Clint suggested. A simple look into his face was enough to convince her that the overwhelming release of their lovemaking had been enough to banish whatever demons were chasing him, at least temporarily.

She knew it couldn't be this way forever. They'd have to return to Timmins tomorrow night, collect Heather from her weekend stay at the MacDonalds's, and try to figure out where to go with their relationship. But for now, she was going to enjoy the moment, and follow Clint's lead in putting the future on hold.

Despite her best intentions, reality kept creeping in. It intruded first while they were still eating their room-service dinner, propped up on the big bed with pillows behind them, watching the evening movie on TV. It was an old Western that Laurie hadn't seen before. Clint, though, admitted to having caught it several times on late-night reruns. Laurie had to smile at the way he mouthed some of the lines in unison with the tough cowboy on the screen.

"Don't worry about a thing, ma'am," he drawled, his diction slightly slurred by cheese from the nachos they were sharing. "There's nobody you can trust better'n me."

When they'd finished eating, Clint looked at the pile of dishes on the trolley their dinner had arrived on. "This is the life," he said with obvious satisfaction. "No dishes to clean up. No shots to give. No planning ahead what's for breakfast tomorrow."

Laurie looked over at him. He *did* look pleased with life just at the moment, more pleased than she'd ever seen him looking. She found it bothered her that he was this carefree only when he was away from his daughter and his own home. On the other hand . . .

"The past few months have been pretty hard on you, haven't they?" she asked him.

She might have known he still wouldn't freely admit to how tortured he'd been. But he did go as far as to say, "It hasn't exactly been a picnic. I'm used to being responsible only for myself and my own business. I'm not sure I'm ever going to come to grips with having someone else's life in my hands."

"Not even your own daughter's?" she couldn't help asking.

"Especially my own daughter's." His voice was grim.

"You won't always have this night-and-day responsibility, you know," Laurie reminded him. "Heather's already much more mature about her diabetes."

"Thanks to you," Clint replied. "Before we came to you, things were just going from bad to worse."

"I can't take all the credit, Clint. You and Heather have both changed in the past few weeks."

"At the risk of repeating myself, that's thanks to you, too," he said stubbornly. "We've both needed someone like you in our lives, Laurie. You've pointed out things to both of us that we needed to see, but couldn't."

She knew he'd meant the words as a compliment and part of her was pleased to hear them. But another part was sending her a faint warning signal again, and she knew it came from her own feelings of not wanting to be cast in the role of instant Mom, as she had been once before in her life. Clint was very quick to pass all the credit on to her for the improved relations between him and his daughter. But Laurie wanted to be very careful that he didn't try to pass on more than her share of the responsibilities, too.

"I wonder how Heather's getting along at the Mac-Donalds's," she said, deliberately bringing the conversation back to the subject of his daughter.

"I'm sure she's having a ball. She was already half in love with those little twin girls when I dropped her off there."

"I don't blame her. They're pretty captivating."

"You sound pretty captivated yourself."

He sounded casual, but out of the corner of her eye Laurie could see him watching her. "I've always liked kids," she said lightly. "Especially little blond ones with blue eyes." He didn't move, but she felt him tense a little. "What about you?" she added.

"What about me and kids, you mean? We get along all right."

She knew his elaborate casualness was covering up his real feelings. And a flicker in his blue eyes reminded her that he didn't want to talk about the future right now. She wondered, with a sudden pang, if he'd ever want to talk about a future that might include blond, blue-eyed children that happened to be his own. At the moment, she was inclined to doubt it.

Their conversation put a damper on the effervescent mood they'd shared earlier, and they agreed once the movie was over, that they were tired. They turned out the light and lay there, both obviously awake, on separate sides of the king-size bed. Laurie felt more alone than she ever had with Clint, wondering if even the hint of possibly sharing his life with her had driven him away.

Then, just as she was about to move toward him for reassurance, he shifted to his side and pulled her wordlessly against him. She found comfort in the strength of his warm embrace, and she wrapped her arms tightly around him as if answering his unspoken plea that she be patient with what they were building together. It wasn't something that could be forced. There were too many problems buried in both their pasts for that. And for the present, this intense longing was more than enough.

As Clint impatiently pushed aside the blanket that covered them, Laurie half expected to feel that same crazy spiraling of sensual pressure that had filled their lovemaking earlier. But it was a surprise to find out just how slow and gentle their pace could be now. It was as though they'd already discovered where their whirlwind attraction for each other could lead, in that one wild climax, and now both of them were intent on deepening the bond that united them, bridging the gaps that mere words hadn't been able to cross yet.

Laurie had never imagined that a man could induce the hazy, half-drugged splendor that filled her limbs when Clint fulfilled his fantasy of kissing her from head to toe. He was maddeningly slow in his movements, heightening her desire for him with each new caress until she writhed in his grip like a spring-loaded machine that he'd set in motion.

His hands had already learned what pleased her most, and it was impossible for Laurie to think of anything else when he coaxed such a vivid response out of the sweet center of her being. She surprised herself with the boldness of her answering caresses, and her own certainty of exactly how he longed to be touched. She felt her own passion growing by quantum leaps when she heard him give the same sharp cries of satisfaction that he'd already torn from her own throat.

But even as she was letting her hands roam over his glorious male body, feeling the springiness of the tawny hair on his chest, the taut muscles of his stomach, the hard length of his desire for her—even then he seemed able to distract her, to make her feel every sensation known to woman. He was insistent, probing, unerringly certain what would drive her wild.

And he pushed her toward that pleasurable place until Laurie gave in and let herself go with that desperate pulsing, crying out as everything in her convulsed and contracted again and again, and then gradually subsided.

By the time her vision cleared, she was more than ready to feel him inside her again. She was so consumed by the magic of their lovemaking that this time she barely spared a thought to his quick, private ritual of making sure they were protected. And the instant he began that slow dance of erotic pleasure again, she was lost to any thoughts but a kind of lazy amazement that she'd never even suspected the depths of pleasure her own body could give her.

Clint seemed determined to make slow love to her the whole night, but suddenly, with an unexpected shift in their position, both of them were caught up again in the roaring tide that had engulfed them before. Their movements quickened, became urgent, became unbearable, and then pushed them one more time into that dark, heated void where all their words and doubts became meaningless.

Afterward, listening to Clint's gradually slowing breaths beside her in the dark, Laurie was content just to think of how much she loved him. He had become such an integral part of her since she'd met him.

It was only when she stirred restlessly in the middle of the night that her unspoken worries came back. She did what they'd promised each other not to do this weekend: she tried looking into the future, to see what it might hold for Clint and her. She wanted a home and a family, with a man who had no qualms about shouldering his share of the responsibility. And Clint, if his words of a few hours ago were to be trusted, wanted less responsibility, not more. He seemed to see his daughter's illness as an ordeal he had to survive, not an opportunity for him to overcome his own poisoned memories of family life.

Laurie willed herself to let the dark thoughts go for the moment, and lulled herself back to sleep by listening to the slow, restful sound of Clint's breathing beside her. He was so tired, she thought. And so was she. Hoping that what they'd shared tonight would outlast their whirlwind trip to the city, she let herself slide back into sleep.

Eight

"**D**o you realize it's anatomically impossible for a person to have feet as cold as yours?"

Laurie blinked her eyes, adjusting to the light in the room. "Anatomically?" she repeated. "That's too long a word for first thing in the morning."

She heard Clint's chuckle, and opened her eyes wider to see him leaning on one elbow and watching her. "In actual fact, it's eleven o'clock already," he said. "We've been sleeping in. And you're missing the point."

Laurie flexed her toes. In spite of the warm hotel room and all the blood-churning exercise she'd had during the night, her feet *were* cold. "Sorry," she said. "They always get a bit cold on winter nights, unless I wear socks to bed." She warmed them on Clint's shins, and felt him flinch in response.

"Saying your toes are a *bit* cold is like saying winter in Timmins is a bit long," he grumbled. She could hear the teasing behind the words, and kept her frigid toes against his warm skin.

"My knees are cold, too," she told him.

He held up a protesting hand. "Let's deal with one disaster area at a time," he said. "Now that you're awake, what do you think about ordering some breakfast?"

"Hmm. I'm not sure I'm quite ready for breakfast yet. We did eat a lot of dinner last night, after all."

"I see what you mean." What she really meant had nothing to do with food. The luxurious way her body was moving against his under the covers was demonstrating her meaning. Clint breathed in slowly, already drowning in the desire that had sprung into life the instant he'd awakened to find Laurie's soft, curvaceous body next to his in the big bed.

Now he stroked her shoulder, loving the satiny smoothness of her skin. "I guess I could be persuaded to put off breakfast for a little while," he said. "After all, we do have to do something to warm up those toes of yours."

Her toes were thoroughly warm by the time they called for breakfast to be sent up to their room. In fact, she felt as though she would never be cold again, and it had nothing to do with the setting on the hotel's thermostat.

That blissful feeling lasted until she sat up in bed, arms around her knees, and let her eyes feast on that athletic body she couldn't imagine ever having enough of. She traced a hand over his hard chest, the curling hairs that seemed to want to wrap themselves around her fingers, the rib cage that rose and fell a little quicker when she touched him, the unobtrusive scar on his right side...

She paused at the scar. She hadn't noticed it before, probably because she'd been too busy being bowled over by the full effect of him to dwell on details. Now she ran a gentle hand down his side, and couldn't help asking, "Where did that scar come from, Clint?"

He seemed startled at her question. "An old war wound," he said flippantly.

His tone didn't fool her. "From the war with your father, you mean?"

That got him up to a half-sitting position, resting on his elbows. "I thought we weren't going to talk about the past this weekend," he said. The harshness of his tone surprised her, and she decided not to press the point.

After their breakfast had arrived and they'd eaten, showered and dressed, though, Clint seemed to recognize that his sharply delivered answer had once again strained the mood between them. With a sigh, he returned to the subject, as though he wanted to clear it up once and for all.

"That scar is a reminder of the time I was hooked up to a lot of tubes and things when I was sixteen," he said bluntly, sitting down on the small sofa in the room. He stretched his legs out in front of him, as though a casual posture could soften what he was describing. "I had a lot of internal injuries, I gather."

Laurie's eyes were gentle, inquiring. He didn't want to share this with her, he found. She was so many worlds away from his hellish boyhood. And yet keeping it to himself all these years had cost him a lot—how much, he was just beginning to realize.

"What started the fight?" she wanted to know.

"I had had an offer I thought I couldn't refuse. A guy in town offered me a job at a lumberyard, and a place to live in exchange for being his night watchman. It would have given me a chance to get away from my home, and enough money to see me through high school."

"How did that sit with your father?"

"Not well. This sounds crazy, Laurie, but—well, he loved me, the same as I loved him. I was all he had. And he didn't want to see me go, even though he knew why I wanted to get away. When I told him I was leaving, he went crazy."

"Did you fight back?"

"Not at first. My dad was a big guy, but he didn't look after himself much. Once I got to be as tall as he was, I'd taken to outrunning him rather than stay and be beaten. But this time, he lit into me like nothing I'd ever seen before. I kept trying to reason with him. I had a stupid, teen-aged idea that he and I should settle things once and for all. But he wasn't playing by any rules I knew, and he kept at me no matter what I said or how hard I tried to keep out of his way. It turned into a brawl, the kind nobody wins."

He felt his heartbeat accelerate as he talked, and saw some of his own recollected fear mirrored in Laurie's eyes. Damn it, he hadn't wanted to get her involved in this. Why did she keep pushing him this way?

"I missed the end of it," he said, wanting to wrap up the story as quickly as he could. "I was unconscious when he loaded me into the cab of the truck and drove me to the hospital."

"I know," Laurie said. Her voice sounded strained, too. "I read the piece about it in the paper."

"I wish you hadn't done that," he said. "How could you possibly understand, from a three-paragraph story written over twenty years ago?"

"It just gave me the facts, Clint. I was waiting to hear the real story from you."

He clamped down on his anger, knowing it was mostly himself he was angry at for having to drag the whole ugly business up again. "Well, I'm almost finished telling it," he said. "When I came to, I knew I couldn't go back home. And I didn't want to stay in Timmins, either. As soon as they'd let me out of the hospital, I emptied out my bank account and hitchhiked to the nearest Canadian Forces base to enlist."

"And your father?"

Clint's hands clenched into fists, without him willing them to. "He roared out of the hospital parking lot and wrapped his truck around the first convenient tree. They chalked it up to drunk driving, but personally, I've always thought he committed suicide.''

He shut his eyes against the memories, feeling as though he'd just ripped the cover off the black, gaping hole inside of him. It was a physical shock when he felt Laurie's hands on his shoulders, and realized she'd crossed the room almost soundlessly to kneel in front of the sofa where he sat.

"I'm glad you told me this, Clint," she said. Her voice was low and full of comfort.

His arms went around her automatically. "Well, it explains the scar, at least," he said. He wished his voice would behave. He wished he could hold Laurie like this forever.

She seemed in no hurry to move. "It explains a lot more than that and you know it," she said.

Her skin smelled faintly of the soap she'd used in the shower a little while ago. He buried his face in her still-damp hair. When she was in his arms, he found he could actually believe in happy endings.

"It explains why you've made yourself so strong in so many ways," she was going on. "Now I understand what you meant when you said you needed defenses against the world. And now I understand why you moved back to Timmins."

He liked the single-minded concentration he heard in her voice. If anyone could understand, it was Laurie Houston, he thought. "And why *did* I move back to Timmins?" he challenged her. She was gently massaging the back of his neck as she held him, and the soothing motion was threatening to distract him.

"To prove you'd survived. To come back to the place you'd left at such a low point, and contrast the successful man you are now with the unhappy kid you were then."

"They make you take obligatory psychology classes at nurse's college, don't they?"

"You're only teasing me because you know I'm right," she replied.

He raised his head and grinned at her. "I just like keeping you know-it-all medical professionals in your place," he said.

"My place? And where is that?"

"At the moment, I think it's over here."

Clint tightened his arms around her and effortlessly swung her onto the sofa beside him. In the same smooth motion, he shifted his body until he was half covering her. This time, the need he felt to bury himself in her was fired by something different and unexpected, something that seemed to come from a new lightness inside. He'd let the light in to a place that had been dark for so many years. And he knew the old wounds wouldn't heal overnight, but for the first time in twenty years he was feeling as though trust—and love—might be things he could reach for after all.

Laurie watched the ground getting closer as the small private plane was about to land in Timmins. "The snow doesn't seem to have melted while we were gone," she sighed.

Clint put a hand over hers. "We were only away thirty-six hours," he reminded her. "Spring thaw in Timmins takes a little longer than that."

"I know. It just seems like we were gone a lot longer, somehow." Laurie looked from his blue eyes to the bleak evening landscape below them, and added, "We never did get to that Greek restaurant, did we?"

In fact, the only sights they'd seen in Toronto had been from the window of their hotel room. "Would you rather have been restaurant-hopping than doing what we were doing?" Clint wanted to know.

His smile had a new warmth to it, and Laurie smiled back. "Not for the world," she said.

"Good. And don't worry about the Greek restaurant. There will be lots more chances to get there." Clint let go of her hand and leaned back in his seat, looking completely at ease. "I'm beginning to remember that there *is* more to life than diets and shots and rules. Now that I've rediscovered it, I'm going to make some changes in the way Heather and I have been living."

"What kinds of changes?" Laurie was curious.

"I don't think it's been good for me to devote every waking hour—and some that should have been spent sleeping—worrying about my daughter's health."

"I'd agree with that," Laurie said. "It does give you a skewed perspective on life."

"Right. Plus, I'd become used to doing my business by phone, or by having people come to me. This weekend has reminded me of how productive it can be to travel, to see what other people are doing, just to get back into the swing of things again. And now that I've got you to help, maybe I don't have to feel quite so tied down to my home base anymore."

Laurie wished she could sort out what she was feeling. On the one hand, he was absolutely right: a monastic life, devoted entirely to keeping his daughter healthy, wasn't a natural one for either Clint or Heather. On the other hand, she remembered Heather's comments about what a jetsetter her father used to be. And he'd included Laurie in the equation, without really asking her how she felt about it. Now that he'd reminded himself what it felt like to have his freedom, how far would he go in trying to recapture it?

"You know, I think we're getting better at this."

Clint looked up in surprise at his daughter's words. He'd been lost in thought, going through the familiar motions of giving Heather her insulin injection while his mind was replaying Laurie's goodbye of earlier this evening. He'd asked her to come home with him after he'd picked up

Heather from the MacDonalds's house, and had been surprised by her polite refusal; she'd said that she was a little tired and wanted to clean up her place before she started another week.

"Since when are you so interested in housework?" he'd demanded, when he'd pulled his gleaming Volvo into her driveway and walked her to the door.

Her eyes had had uncertainty in them, and he hadn't liked that. "All right, I'll be honest," she'd said. "It's not just the housework, although there *are* things in the back of my fridge that could probably rival any antibiotic ever discovered. But I thought you and Heather might want to have some time by yourselves, that's all."

"We'd both love to have you around," he said stubbornly. "You know I would, anyway."

Even that statement hadn't chased away the uncertainty in her eyes. Laurie turned her key in the front door lock and reached to take her overnight bag from Clint's hand. "I'll talk to you tomorrow," she said. "Give me a call around lunchtime, and I'll probably be in."

Clint had refused to hand her the suitcase until he'd been given a hug. "It's like hugging a snowman," he commented, when he'd pulled her against him.

"I knew my system would go into shock, coming back here after that warm hotel room," Laurie said, when they'd separated. "So I put on all the clothes I had." She tilted an ear in the direction of her front hall, and added, "Hear that? My refrigerator really is calling me. I'll talk to you tomorrow, okay?"

And then she'd gone in. Two hours later as he and his daughter measured out the correct insulin dose, Clint was still puzzling over Laurie's reluctance to come home with him and Heather. Heather's comment that they were getting better at this recalled him to the present.

"We should be," he replied. "We've had enough practice."

Heather actually giggled. "I guess so," she said. "It's funny. At first I thought Dr. MacDonald was better at giving shots than you are. But now I think he's not."

"What makes you say that?" The idea that his daughter actually appreciated his carefully learned new skills captured Clint's full attention for the moment, banishing his thoughts of Laurie.

"You get it over with quicker, for one thing." Heather giggled again. "And you're just—I don't know, more comfortable with it."

Trying to appear calm and comfortable while giving someone an injection had been one of the hardest things Clint had ever had to learn to do. He smiled back at his daughter, warmed by her compliment.

"Thanks," he said. "Wait till you see my bill."

Heather assumed a lofty air. "Oh, I don't deal with anything as mundane as bills," she said, waving her free arm in the air. "My secretaries handle all of that."

"More than one secretary? You must be a big deal."

"Oh, I am. A very big deal."

The injection over with, Clint started to put away their equipment. "Sounds as though you had a good weekend at Dr. MacDonald's," he said. "You're in a pretty bubbly mood."

The look she gave him was more knowing than he'd thought a fifteen-year-old could be. "Sounds as though *your* weekend was pretty good, too," she said. "How come Laurie didn't want to come home with us?"

So he *hadn't* gotten away from the subject, after all. "I'm not sure, honey," he said. "I think she was just tired."

"I guess you guys did a lot of sight-seeing," Heather said. Her face was suspiciously innocent.

Clint frowned at her. "Some," he said. This was all new to him. How far did a father go in discussing his love life with his teenaged daughter? From the unaccustomed gleam in Heather's eye, it was apparent he wasn't coming across with as many details as she would have liked him to.

"Let's invite her to dinner this week," Heather went on enthusiastically. "I'll cook."

Cooking was a safe subject, surely. "Sounds fine to me," Clint said. "What are you going to make?"

Heather frowned, concentrating. "How about that lamb stuff Mom used to make?" she asked. "That was always my favorite. We haven't had it since that night you—" She stopped, and bit off what she'd been about to say. "Or maybe I'll make something else, instead," she finished lamely.

Clint knew exactly what night she'd been referring to. Shortly after Heather's diabetes had been diagnosed, Clint had made lamb stew, a favorite recipe of Heather's mother. It had been a special treat for the girl, a way of trying to reconcile her to her new diet. But after school that day, Heather had been caught up in an expedition suggested by one of her friends, and she'd been hours late for dinner. By then, Clint had been jumping out of his skin with worry. He'd called her friends' parents, who had also confessed to some anxiety about their daughters' whereabouts, and that hadn't helped any. Memories of the trouble Heather had gotten into in Toronto, and fear about what forbidden foods she might be eating and what the effect of that might be, had made him pretty sharp with her when she'd finally walked in the door.

"Things are different now, honey," he said slowly, remembering the lamb stew that both of them had been too upset to eat. "Maybe it's time to try that recipe again."

She looked up at him, and he felt the weight of her assessing stare. "I was scared of you that night," she said bluntly.

Her words hit him like a jolt in the stomach, but he was glad she was being so direct with him. "I remember," he said.

"The night before that, I thought we were getting along so well," she went on. Her voice was small, but determined. "I got an *A* on my science project, remember? The one you helped me with? And you were so happy about it."

Clint fought an urge to sink his face into his hands. He didn't want to tell her everything, but there were some things she needed to know.

"Sugar, there's something you have to understand about me," he said, looking into her face. "When I was your age, my father went from one extreme to the other almost every day, first building me up and then tearing me down. Sometimes the way he did it was pretty rough."

"Rough? You mean he hit you?"

"I'm afraid so. I'll spare you the gory details. But the result is that I was scared when I heard myself starting to do the same thing with you—praising you one day and wanting to wallop you the next."

She picked up on the least likely part of what he said. "You were scared?" She sounded as if she suspected he was kidding her.

"Shaking in my boots. Because the last thing on earth I wanted to do was repeat the mistakes my father made with me. And that's why—" Clint cleared his throat, knowing he wasn't sounding at all as adult and in command as he wanted to be. "That's why I've sometimes seemed a little distant with you, honey. I had this sneaking suspicion that if I got too close, I might find myself doing and saying things I never wanted to do or say."

Light was dawning on Heather's fair-skinned face. "Like the lamb stew night, when I came in late," she said. "You were so mad, and then all of a sudden you weren't."

Clint remembered it, agonizingly. Heather had yelled at him that she could do what she pleased, and he'd shouted back that she couldn't, not while she lived under his roof. And then, like a black lightning bolt, he'd remembered his father shouting exactly those words at him, just before their final and decisive fight. It was as if a ghost had walked into the room. Clint had clamped down hard, then, and forced himself to concentrate on the impersonal details of testing Heather's blood sugar and calculating her insulin dosage, refusing to give in to his own anger.

But now, as they talked about it, he knew she was finally starting to understand. And he knew that wouldn't have happened if he hadn't made Laurie understand first. She'd been the first person he'd felt he could open up to, the first woman to coax those long-buried feelings out of hiding.

Then why had she been so distant this evening? Clint was still bothered by her almost-cool goodbye, but he told himself he'd sort it out with her tomorrow. In the meantime, the affectionate good-night hug his daughter gave him almost made up for the fact that when he settled into his own bed that night, Laurie wasn't in it with him.

The lamb stew smelled delicious. It was a pity Laurie hadn't had much appetite this week.

It was Thursday, four days after she and Clint had flown back from Toronto. He'd called her on Monday, as he'd promised, and invited her to dinner on Thursday evening. "Heather's cooking," he'd said, with a pleased chuckle.

"Sounds as if she *did* talk herself into a permanent job," Laurie commented.

"Well, a part-time one, at least. Now that I don't *have* to cook three meals a day every day, I find I sort of miss being the cook."

In spite of their good-natured banter, Laurie felt uneasy about the conversation. Clint had dropped that last-angry-man pose that she'd desperately wanted him to get past and that was good. But now he seemed to have gone from shunning her help to assuming casually that she'd settle right into his and Heather's daily lives. And that made her wary. It was just too soon for them to have made this quantum leap. It felt strange, after all her urging that Clint get over his unhappy memories, to find that her own past was now rising up to haunt her.

Still, she'd accepted his invitation to dinner on Thursday night. And when she'd arrived, with a still-warm loaf of fresh bread tucked into the crook of her arm, she'd found Heather racing around the kitchen in a cooking frenzy, but no Clint.

"He had to meet somebody downtown," Heather explained, stirring a pot on the stove with one hand and searching through the spice rack with the other. "He said he'll be home soon. Now, if you were my father, where would you have hidden the paprika?"

Laurie managed to find Clint's hiding place for the paprika, but her real attention was elsewhere. Clint still wasn't home by the time she and Heather were ready to sit down to eat.

"He said to go ahead without him if we were hungry," Heather said. "And I'm starved. How about you?"

Laurie didn't want to admit to the knot she felt in her throat. She helped Heather set the table, and the two of them sat down to the stew Heather had made. It was a good thing the girl was in such a good mood, Laurie thought, because she herself didn't feel like much of a dinner companion at the moment.

She wished Clint weren't doing this to her. The situation was far too reminiscent of too many evenings in Laurie's youth, when her hardworking father had called to say he wouldn't be home until later, and Laurie and her brothers should go ahead and eat without him. She hadn't minded the cooking, but she'd never become accustomed to the feeling of being left on her own to deal with the questions and demands and problems—yes, and even the boisterous affection—of two younger brothers.

"Dr. MacDonald said I could baby-sit for his little girls someday," Heather was saying, full of enthusiasm. "Aren't they cute, Laurie?"

"Very cute," Laurie agreed. "And pretty much of a handful, too."

"I know. One of them got hold of an English paper I was working on, and decorated it with green crayon. I'm going to tell my teacher it was Shakespeare coming back from the dead and trying to dictate a new play." Heather grinned, then added, "Do you have nieces and nephews, Laurie?"

"Two nieces. My youngest brother is a bachelor, but the middle one, in Toronto, has a two-year-old and a one-year-old."

"Did you see them when you were there last weekend?"

"No. There wasn't time. We talked on the phone, though."

Laurie felt the knot inside her tighten a little. Last weekend she'd been utterly absorbed by Clint and their growing need for each other. But now, even the mention of her younger brothers conjured up unresolved feelings in her.

What was she getting into here? Was it a replay of the situation she'd resented so much ten years ago? Was Laurie again being cast as someone's mother without even being consulted about it? Before she could answer the question in her own mind, Clint walked in the door, stamping the snow off his feet and filling the room, as always, with his larger-than-life presence.

He apologized for being late, as he took off his sheepskin coat and sat down at the table. Laurie gave him a couple of points for the apology; it was something her father had seldom bothered to do. Still, when her eyes met Clint's across the table, she still felt worry along with the now-familiar little jolt of desire for him. He was so handsome, so cavalier, and so maddeningly silent about what was really going on in his mind.

She had to wait until after dinner, when Heather was downstairs doing her homework, to talk to him alone. And then, it seemed, he had other things on his mind besides talking. As she rose to clear the table, he captured her in his arms and pulled her to him, murmuring against her ear how glad he was to see her.

In spite of all her unanswered questions, Laurie felt herself move willingly into his embrace, warmed and comforted just for the moment by the invisible bond between them.

"You don't know how much it meant to me to come in that door tonight and see you sitting at my kitchen table as if you'd belonged there all your life," he was saying. The words were a soft rumble that set up a vibration in her nervous system, and it took a long moment for Laurie to sift through what he'd really said.

She pulled her head back slightly and looked at him. The satisfaction on his face was evident. His wide lips had curved into a smile, and the tightly clenched air was gone from his expression. Only his blue eyes kept some of the watchfulness she'd noticed in him at the very beginning. It made her think things weren't quite as simple as he was implying they were.

"I'm glad to see you, too, Clint," she said. "But I have to admit, it made me a little nervous when Heather said you'd be late because you got held up at work."

"Nervous? Why?"

Laurie sighed. When she was in his arms like this, it was hard to think clearly. All she wanted to do was give in to his strength and the subtle pulse of desire that she could still feel in spite of all her reservations. But it was important that he know how she felt.

"I already told you about the way I got stuck being mother to my two younger brothers," she said. "Maybe I didn't tell you emphatically enough just how much I resented it at times."

"You don't think I'm trying to do the same thing, do you?" There was an edge to his voice.

When he phrased it that bluntly, she had to wonder at herself. Was she letting her past control her judgment, the way Clint had done until recently?

"I just wanted to make sure you weren't," she said finally, still not sure. "Sitting down at the table with one parent missing has too many associations for me, that's all."

"Well, I think Heather got a big kick out of it," he said, pulling her closer again so that she could feel the beat of his heart. "After having just me to look at across the table at every meal for the past couple of years, I think she loved having some company of her own."

Is that why you invited me? Laurie wanted to ask. To be company for Heather? She knew there was more to it than that—knew it intimately from the way he kissed the base of her neck at her open-collared blouse, and let his knowing hands rove over every curve of her body as he held her tight. But she needed more reassurance than that, and for some reason, Clint wasn't giving it to her.

What he *was* giving her was heart palpitations. He turned his attention to her lips, coaxing a response from her in a way that banished all her troubled thoughts. She returned his kiss hungrily, wanting to lose herself in the sweetness of his caresses. But that nagging little voice in her mind wouldn't go away.

It surfaced again when he finally broke their embrace and said, "I got a lucky break tonight."

"Is that what your meeting was about?"

"Yes. I've owned some property outside of Montreal for years, and I've been waiting for the right project to come along to develop it. One of the people I met in Toronto last weekend has a proposal that seems perfect."

"That's good, Clint." She watched him closely. "Will that mean traveling to Montreal a lot?"

"Well, not yet. We're still in the early stages. But eventually, yes." The lighter centers of his blue eyes lit with a mischievous gleam. "Interested in a weekend in Montreal with me?"

He seemed surprised when she didn't match the suggestiveness of his tone. "What about Heather?" she asked. "If you're going to be spending more time traveling, you'll need to think about that."

He seemed annoyed. "I've thought of it, of course," he said. "Since Heather's been doing so much better lately, I'm hoping she'll be able to look after herself when I'm away for the odd weekend. Or would that be against doctor's orders?"

To her dismay, she heard an echo of his earlier statement at her "interfering" in their lives. She spoke quickly, wanting to soften that impression. "No, it's not against doctor's orders," she said. "I guess I was just remembering Heather talking about the old days, when you were on the road all the time. I was wondering if you were headed back in that direction."

She had a feeling part of his annoyance was at himself. "Laurie, for two years I've been working entirely in Timmins. For the past four months I've barely set foot out of my own home. And now that I see a little elbow room, and a chance to take up my life where I left off—a life, I might add, that I enjoyed—I'd have to think twice before I passed up the opportunity."

"I can understand that," she said in a neutral voice. She could, too. That was the hell of it. "I'm just trying to see where Heather fits into this. And me." *And us*, she might have added, but didn't.

"I'll tell you exactly where you fit in," he said. "You're the one who's made it possible for me even to think about expanding my horizons again. Until I met you, I had the feeling I had to do all of this on my own, without help from anyone." His words were blunt, and she could hear the sincerity in them. "You've shown me that I can accept help, and loosen my hold, without losing the things that are important to me. And now you don't seem to like the results."

Laurie put her hands on her hips, exasperated with the man. He seemed to be able to take her simplest question and twist it into something complicated. Or maybe it was her own lack of certainty that was doing that.

"I'm just trying to see how this is going to work, in practical terms," she insisted. "If you're away a lot, Heather's going to be lonely. How do you plan on handling that?"

Clint, too, looked exasperated. "But we've got you to help now," he said, as if she was missing the obvious answer. "You've become a part of this family, Laurie. Surely you must feel that, just as much as Heather and I do."

"So I'm supposed to take up the slack in helping you be a parent to Heather," Laurie said slowly, and with growing resentment. "What happened to the offer of a passionate weekend in Montreal? I can't be two people, Clint, not even for you."

As she spoke, she knew exactly what the problem was. Clint *was* asking her to be two separate people; Laurie his lover, the woman he'd opened up to after all these years. And Laurie the member of his family, the one who would be happy to be there for Heather when he couldn't be. She was pretty sure it was too tall an order for her to fill.

"Exactly how do you envision this working out, Clint?" she pushed him, honestly wanting to know. "It all seems a little vague to me at the moment."

From the shrug he gave, it was obvious he was as uncertain as she was. "You were the one who wanted me to stop being so obsessive about planning everything," he said. "Or have you changed your mind on that point?"

Laurie shook her head slowly. "I just don't think winging it is what's called for right now," she said. "And I don't want us to slide into habits that end up hurting all three of us."

Both of them seemed unwilling to pursue the subject any further for the moment, but there was an uneasy sense that it would come up again before too long. And in spite of the lingering passion in their kisses, Laurie knew it would be a mistake to stay with Clint tonight. For one thing, they were back to being chaperoned again, with Heather dutifully doing her homework two rooms away.

And for another, she'd been right that there would be plenty of reality to face once they'd come back from their escapist weekend in Toronto. As she said good-night to Clint, momentarily reveling in the all-consuming strength of his embrace, she hoped against hope that what they felt for each other was strong enough to push through the obstacles that still seemed to surround them.

Nine

"Guess what, Laurie?" Nelson's eyes were shining with a glow that seemed entirely inappropriate for first thing on a Monday morning. Laurie paused in the act of taking off her coat.

"You look like you've won the lottery," she said.

"Better than that." Her secretary waved an official-looking letter at her. "I got accepted at engineering school—my first choice, no less!"

"Nelson, that's wonderful." Laurie scanned the letter he held out to her. "And they're giving you that scholarship, too."

"Isn't it great? But that's not the best part. You know how set my parents were against me going to university?"

Laurie remembered. Nelson's parents had the notion that anything beyond a high school education was a waste of time for their son and had refused to help the boy further his ambitions for an engineering career. It wasn't until Laurie had offered him a job as her secretary that he'd been able to think about saving enough money to fulfill his dream.

"Well, when I showed them this, I think they finally started to take me seriously. They realized that I'm going to school anyway, with or without their help, so now they're willing to chip in."

"Nelson, I'm so happy for you that I'm not even going to let myself think how much I was looking forward to having you as my secretary for another year," Laurie said.

His young face sobered a bit at that. "I feel sort of bad, leaving you a year earlier than I said I would," he admitted.

Laurie shook her head at him. "I was just kidding," she said, "although I *will* miss you. But I'm thrilled at your news."

"I never would have made it this far if you hadn't taken a chance on me, Laurie," he said, suddenly getting sentimental on her. "I didn't even know how to type when you took me on."

"Give me some credit, Nelson," she laughed. "I could tell what an organizational genius you were the moment you walked in here asking for a job. Anybody can learn to type."

He refused to let her joke about it. "Well, I'm serious," he said. "You're the one who's made this really possible, and I'll always remember that."

As she headed into her inner office a few minutes later, Laurie found herself strangely disturbed by Nelson's words. They were too much of an echo of what Clint had said on Thursday night. Was it selfish of her to feel tired of always being the one people called on for help? Laurie knew she had always had a giving nature, but just at the moment it was feeling strained to the limit.

The intercom on her desk buzzed, and she pushed the button to hear Nelson's voice announcing that her first patient of the day was here. "Oh, and I forgot to tell you," he added. "There was a message on the machine this morning from a Dr. Malcolm in Toronto. I'll put the number in your box, okay?"

"Great. I'll call her back as soon as I'm free." Laurie was pleased at the idea of talking to Sarah Malcolm, a well-respected nutritionist in the city who'd been one of Laurie's mentors at school. The notion brightened her mood considerably, and she started her working day determined not to dwell on either the problem of replacing Nelson or figuring out what to do about Clint.

Clint could feel his muscles urging him to dive, eager for the exercise of swimming his daily half mile. He tensed his thighs, ready to push himself off the end of the pool and into the heated water, but then paused trying to identify what was bothering him.

It didn't take too much thought to recognize that it was Laurie who was on his mind. He couldn't swim in his own pool now without being overcome by images of her, the way she'd looked in the slick aquamarine suit he'd bought her, or how her face had softened and glowed in the passion of their weekend together in Toronto.

Damn it, that was a week and a half ago, already. And he'd been hungering for her ever since, needing to renew the intimacy and warmth they'd shared. He wasn't fool enough to think that he could change his whole way of going about things all at once, but he did know that he needed Laurie's help if he was going to change at all.

He relaxed his tightly corded muscles and walked barefoot over to the phone in the living room. Just sitting down on the sofa recalled the night they'd lain here together, with Laurie in her old nightgown and mismatched socks. He breathed in deeply and dialed her number from memory.

"Hello, this is Laurie. I'm sorry I can't come to the phone right now..."

Clint cursed the answering machine fluently, and, fortunately for Laurie's ears, before the beep. After the tone,
he spoke more sedately. "Laurie, this is Clint. Give me a
call when you get in, okay?"

He went back to his exercise routine, but part of him was
half listening for the phone, and when it rang, sixteen pool
lengths into his workout, he heard it immediately. He was
out of the water and into the living room in an instant, not
worrying about the drips on the floor that his towel
couldn't catch.

"Hi, Clint."

He let out a deep breath at the sound of her voice.
"Laurie. Thanks for calling back."

"You sound out of breath. Where were you?"

"In the pool."

"Oh." Did the change in her tone mean she, too, was remembering the day they'd swum together in the warm pool,
and the way the conspiratorial waters had rocked them into
the embrace both of them had been longing for?

Clint cleared his throat. "I have a proposition for you,"
he said.

"That sounds enticing."

"Well, I hope it is. I'm going to make a quick trip to
Montreal, just over Friday night."

There was disappointment in her voice. "Clint, I can't
come along. I have a friend coming in from out of town,
and—"

"Actually, the proposition involves *Saturday* night. I was
hoping I could talk you into staying here with Heather on
Friday, and then on Saturday, when I come home, we can
do something together, all three of us."

There was a long pause. Clint had the feeling he'd blown
it somehow. Why wasn't he better at this?

Because he'd had no practice at fitting a new person into
his life, that was why. The only romantic involvements he'd
had in the past dozen years had been temporary flings, un-

derstood as such by both sides. With Laurie, he was trying not to rush things, trying to go one step at a time. Inviting her to share their day-to-day life seemed like a logical first step. But why did she sound so hesitant when she finally answered?

"Sorry, Clint," she said. "This out-of-town friend is a doctor who's here for a meeting at the hospital. She's asked me to go to the meeting with her to help demonstrate some things and I've accepted."

Clint backpedaled in a hurry. He didn't like being turned down. It made him feel he'd had no right to ask in the first place. Besides, she had a perfectly valid reason for saying no.

"Sounds like something you don't want to miss," he said mechanically.

"It *is* a good opportunity to learn some things," she agreed. "What about Heather? Will you be able to find someone else to stay with her?"

"Sure." He found himself wanting to end the conversation. "Or she can stay by herself. She's doing a lot better at policing what she eats."

"I know she is." Again there was that hesitation. "I'm sorry, Clint."

"No reason to be." Under his light tone he was trying to hide his unexpected sense of having been abandoned by the one person he'd thought he could count on. The thought made him edgy.

They chatted inconsequentially for a few moments, about Clint's upcoming business and Heather's school play, but there was still a feeling of unease when they hung up. "Damn!" Clint said under his breath. He flipped the towel off his neck with a sudden movement, snapping it with a satisfyingly sharp noise in the air. Still frowning, he headed back to the pool and started into a second half mile.

* * *

Dr. Sarah Malcolm had brought with her the apparatus for a new and still controversial method of testing for food allergies. She had it set up in Laurie's living room, and the two of them were working through the presentation Sarah was planning to give tomorrow at the hospital. Laurie was sure it was fascinating, but she couldn't keep her mind on it for two minutes at a time.

"What's the matter, Laurie?" Sarah finally asked, sitting back on Laurie's comfortable sofa. "You seem distracted."

"Blame it on the fact that it's Friday," Laurie said, with a little laugh. "I'm always a bit tired by the end of the week."

Especially when I've spent the week thinking about a certain blond gentleman who's somehow muscled his way into my life and made a big question mark out of it, she almost added. She remembered her very first impression of Clint, storming into her office in his own portable tornado. He'd been doing that ever since, she thought ruefully, and realized that her attention was wandering yet again.

"I'm going to make some tea," she announced, getting to her feet. "Want some?"

Maybe puttering around in her kitchen would help take her mind off Clint. Laurie put the kettle on, and was reaching into the cupboard for her teapot when she heard the pounding at her front door.

"My gracious," Sarah said from the living room. "Do you want me to answer that?"

"No." Laurie gritted her teeth. She had a feeling she knew who her visitor was. "I'll get it."

She was right. Clint stood on her doorstep, hands shoved deep into the pockets of his sheepskin coat. He was glowering at her, as if he'd been dragged here against his will.

"Laurie, believe me, I wouldn't be here if I didn't have to be."

Laurie almost laughed. As an opening remark, it wasn't quite what she'd expected.

"Just the words a girl is always longing to hear," she said. "Come on in."

"No." He planted his boot-shod feet a little more firmly on her porch, as if prepared to resist her physically if that was what it took to stand his ground. "A simple yes or no will do it."

She could see in his eyes that he was expecting "no," and hoping desperately for "yes." The thought made her take a deep breath, as she remembered just how badly Clint had been hurt once by the one person he should have been able to count on. She knew he was counting on her that way now. And because of that, she had to be careful how she answered him.

"Fire away," she said. She stepped out to join him in the frosty night, pulling the door closed behind her to keep the heat in and to give them a little more privacy—although with the porch light shining directly above them, she felt vaguely as though she were being interrogated.

"I told you I have to make a quick run to Montreal," he said tightly. "I was going to leave Heather on her own. But she's picked up a flu bug, and I'm worried about her."

"Can't you stay?" In spite of her resolution to be calm and careful, Laurie felt all her old uneasiness coming back.

"No, I can't." He wasn't going into detail.

"What happened to your policy of making them come to you, when it was your money they were after?" she asked him.

"This is different. This is a cooperative venture, and a very tricky one at that."

The night was cold and very still. Their words hitting the air turned to white clouds, like hints of a storm to come.

Laurie crossed her arms over her chest, feeling chilled in spite of the sweater she was wearing.

"Well, Clint," she said practically, "maybe you'll just have to reschedule the meeting."

She wasn't prepared for the strength of his reaction. He brought a gloved hand down on her porch railing with a force that had to sting, and glared at her with eyes like blue ice.

"I'm talking about one single overnight stay," he said. "I'll be back by tomorrow evening. It's not as though I'm asking for a lifetime commitment."

She wanted to blurt out that she wasn't sure he could handle a lifetime commitment. The thought of sharing everything with Clint, in good times and bad, was a dizzily enticing one. But so far he'd shown no signs of wanting any such thing. Instead, she had an awful feeling that whatever they'd started to build up together was already disintegrating into a series of small favors like this one, favors that would eventually turn passion and trust into resentment.

She'd had enough of that when she was younger. And what she and Clint had was too special to fritter away like that. She hated the thought of letting Heather down, and she wished she could offer aid and comfort. But her instinct for self-preservation told her she had better draw some lines, and fast.

"I'm sorry, Clint," she repeated, wishing her voice sounded firmer. "But Sarah and I have made plans to go out with some colleagues tonight, and we may not be home until quite late. And then tomorrow I'll be tied up all day. I wouldn't be much help to Heather, I'm afraid."

She didn't like the way his blue eyes darkened ominously at her words. "I guess I should have known it was a mistake to try to count on anybody but myself," he muttered. Laurie could hear an echo of the bitter lessons he'd learned so early in his life.

"That's not the point," she said, moving a little closer to him. She didn't like the way he was withdrawing inside himself again. Maybe a little friendly contact would reassure him that she wasn't abandoning him for good.

But he pushed away her offered hand with an authoritative gesture. "Then what *is* the point?" he demanded.

Laurie's sigh turned into a long white cloud that hung in the air between them. "The point is that I don't want to feel I'm at your beck and call whenever you need help with Heather," she said. She knew that wasn't the whole story. But surely he'd get the idea.

He seemed to, and he didn't like it. His arms were crossed again, and the bulk of him in that oversized coat was imposing and a little frightening.

"I told you I wouldn't have asked if there was any way around it," he said stubbornly.

"Any way except rescheduling your meeting, you mean," she shot back at him. She was starting to feel the warming glow of anger now.

"I did try that."

"Did you try calling George MacDonald? Maybe he can suggest someone to stay with Heather."

He waved away the suggestion. "He's out of town."

"What about a temporary nursing agency? I used to work for one of those, and they can be—"

"Overbooked." His eyes were locked on hers.

"Did you try the home care unit at the hospital?" Laurie was racking her brains, trying to avoid the inevitable conclusion that he was forcing on her: he was stuck, and he was trying to push her into bailing him out.

"This doesn't fall into their emergency category," he informed her. "Damn it, Laurie, I've tried everything to avoid asking you this. Can't you see that?"

She could, only too well. She still felt angry, at the whole situation and not just at Clint. They were still so far from sorting out their problems, and here he was pushing her into a replay of the exact situation she'd chafed under from the time she was twelve until she'd wrenched herself free at twenty.

"I'm sorry, Clint," she said huskily. "You're asking the wrong person."

His eyes were full of a hundred conflicting emotions. "What do you mean, the wrong person?" he demanded. "You're the one who got me to the point where I could even think about having a life of my own again," he said. "And now, when I need you, you say you can't be there."

"Stop twisting my words like that," she told him. "I *have* been there to help you—you know that."

"Up till now." His voice was low.

"Yes, because now I have the sneaking feeling we're getting into a pattern of Clint calling Laurie because he needs a favor and good old Laurie feeling like she has to help out. And I don't want that."

What *did* she want? In a sudden flash, she knew she wanted much more from Clint Daniels than either the bewildering passion of their weekend together, or this casual friend-helping-friend arrangement they seemed to have drifted into. *She wanted to share his life with him; she wanted it all.*

And he didn't seem anywhere near ready to give it. His voice was bitter as he said, "All right, I see what's happening."

"Care to let me in on it?"

"Sure. You got stuck being a parent once before when you weren't ready for it. And now you're running away from anything that looks even remotely like the same situation."

She was stung by his words, perhaps because she sensed they were partly true. "For your information, this looks a lot more than *remotely like* what I got stuck with before," she said crisply. "And I wouldn't say I'm running away. I'd say I'm just being darn careful not to get set up that way again.''

''Is that what you think? That I'm setting you up?''

There was real pain in his voice now, and in his eyes. She could hardly bear to look up at him.

''I don't know what to think, Clint,'' she said, as honestly as she could. She wrapped her arms more tightly around herself, shivering a little with more than mere cold. ''I feel that if we're not careful, we're going to come to a dead end.''

''To hell with being careful!''

His words were a sudden snarl, and his movements were so quick she didn't even have time to unfold her arms before he'd pinned her against him. She was suddenly enfolded in the pungent smell of sheepskin the clean, male scent of Clint.

She half struggled in his grip, aware that half of her wanted to protest against his masterful strength, and the other half simply wanted to get her own crossed arms out of the way, so she could be even nearer to him.

''You didn't seem worried about being careful when you came to Toronto with me,'' he said, his voice jagged against her ear. ''Then, you were willing to give in to the moment and just let things happen.''

She should be reasonable, and point out to him that they'd both known that their temporary euphoria couldn't last. But as she tilted her head up to look at him, all she could think of was how she'd loved the thousand and one sensations of giving herself to him. The memory of it was almost palpable, coursing through her with the knife-edged coldness of a mountain stream. The tang and exhilaration of it made her gasp.

''I remember,'' she said shakily.

''Good.'' His voice still sounded rough, as if he was fighting against himself. ''And just in case you've forgotten any minor details—''

She was reaching for his kiss even before he started to claim her lips. She knew one embrace wasn't going to chase away all the doubts that still stood between them. But they kissed as though somehow, their passion could overcome their differences and show them a clear path into the future.

The feeling of their mouths merging was like cold silver meeting sun-warmed gold. The man must have a private generator somewhere in his body, Laurie thought hazily, as her lips opened to him and she felt the warm invasion of his tongue. She could feel the heat radiating from his body even through the thick layer of his coat, and her fingers clutched his shoulders convulsively, consumed with the need to touch him and be touched by him in return.

She heard herself making little hungry sounds that contradicted her practical words of a few minutes ago. And when he lifted his lips slightly and brushed her mouth with his, she said his name on a note of longing that came very close to baring her own soul.

"Oh, Clint..."

His arms tightened around her at her words, and she clung to him in return, reminded irresistibly of the first unexpected hug they'd shared in his kitchen. Then, it had seemed like a gateway to new and unexplored horizons. Now, though, their convulsive embrace felt like an attempt to fight off doubt and the very real fear of losing each other.

They didn't step apart right away, but when Clint said huskily, "Does that make a difference in your thinking?" Laurie knew she had to move. He was just too damn seductive at close range.

"I meant what I said earlier, Clint," she said shakily. "Did you think one kiss would completely change my mind?"

He drew in a long breath, then let it out. The haze of his breath made a bright cloud under Laurie's porch light.

"It must be nice to be so sure of exactly what you want."
There was a sardonic edge to his voice that she didn't like.

"Well, at least I know what I *don't* want," she replied.
"I don't want to be treated like the goddess of love one
moment—" It was true, she realized. That was exactly what
she felt like in Clint's arms. "And then used as a substitute
baby-sitter the next," she finished. "We can't go on this
way, Clint."

What she really wanted, she was sure now, was Clint
himself, his wholehearted love, his everyday life—yes, she
had to admit it, his children, past and present. And he
seemed so far from offering that to her. He'd shied away
from each and every mention of a long-term commitment.

"Maybe it's a mistake to think we can go on, then," he
was saying brusquely. He fastened the top button of his
coat, as if locking himself away from her again. "I have to
go, Laurie. I have a plane to catch."

"What about Heather?" She couldn't help asking.

His eyes glittered in the lamplight. "As you've so elo-
quently pointed out, that's my problem," he said.

He was right, she had. Laurie had never felt so torn in
her life. "I don't want you to think I'm not concerned,"
she began.

"Just that you don't want to be involved. I get the picture." He turned abruptly away, then paused on her top
step and turned back. "Tell me one thing, Laurie. When
you were growing up, and stuck taking care of your brothers, missing a social life and your freedom and the youth
you should have had, did you still love them?"

"Of course." She blinked, taken by surprise by the
question.

He nodded, as if she'd just confirmed something for him.
"I told you love isn't always such a good thing, didn't I?"
he said harshly. And then he was gone, back into the icy
night. Laurie waited until his car had pulled out of the
driveway. Then she went back inside to face her friend's

puzzled looks, knowing that Sarah couldn't possibly be as confused by the whole thing as Laurie was herself.

Darn the telephone, anyway. It wouldn't stop ringing, no matter how hard Laurie tried to stay asleep. She dug herself deeper into the covers, clinging to the end of a dream she'd been having. It was about Clint—all her dreams had been about him, in the three nights since she'd seen him. In this one, he'd been standing at the open door of a small private plane, urging her to hurry or he was going to tell the pilot to leave without her. Her dream-slowed feet had dragged across the tarmac, keeping her from joining him even though she was trying to run.

One more ring of the telephone finally jolted her into waking. It hadn't been a very comforting dream, but at least Clint was in it. She'd been working herself as hard as she could ever since their encounter on Friday night, first with her busy weekend with Sarah Malcolm, and today with an overbooked day of seeing patients, but even trying to satisfy her physical weariness hadn't given her the rest she needed. Only sorting things out with Clint could do that.

The sudden thought that this must be Clint on the telephone cleared the final mists out of her sleepy brain. She rolled over in bed, glancing at the clock. Six o'clock in the morning. Maybe Clint, too, had been unable to sleep these past few nights.

"Hello?" she said, propping herself up on one elbow.

It wasn't Clint. Somehow she knew that even before the stranger's voice answered her.

"Ms. Houston? I'm sorry to wake you so early, but I'm afraid I have bad news."

"Who is this?"

The woman identified herself as an emergency room nurse at Toronto's Western Hospital, and Laurie felt the stab of a sudden and unpleasant memory. She'd had to make these calls herself, when she was a nurse.

"Your brother and sister-in-law were in an accident last night, on their way home from the theater," the nurse was saying, her voice steady with that professional calm Laurie knew so well. She was already sitting up in bed as she listened and asked questions, reaching for her clothes.

Barry and Rhonda were in no immediate danger—that was the first and most important thing. But there had been some serious injuries, and they would have to be in the hospital for a week at least. A neighbor was looking after their two little girls, but only for one night. Barry and Rhonda had expressed the hope that Laurie could come and stay with her nieces, at least for a few days.

"Tell them it's all right," Laurie said. "I'll be there just as soon as I can."

Suddenly there were a hundred things to do. Laurie felt as though her hurried packing happened simultaneously with the phone calls she had to make—to her office answering machine, asking Nelson to reschedule her appointments for the rest of the week, to the airport to see when the next flight was, and to a taxi company to get her there when it turned out there was an early flight leaving soon and she could have a seat on it if she hurried.

There wasn't time to dwell on what she was doing. She got herself together by the time the taxi showed up, and during the ride to the airport she only had time to feel grateful she'd decided not to drive. The roads were clear, but her state of mind definitely was not, and it was a relief to have someone else behind the wheel.

It wasn't until she'd settled down in her seat and taken a deep breath that the situation really came home to her. She looked out the window at the bleak early-morning light, and realized that once again, she was being asked to come to the rescue. And once again, she was all alone.

Ten

"**Y**ou're not eating."

The words made Clint look up in surprise. For the past few months, that had been *his* line. It was strange to hear it coming from his daughter's lips.

She was half teasing him, tossing his own familiar phrases back at him over the dinner table. "I thought this was something you liked," she said, gesturing to his half-eaten ratatouille. "That's why I made it tonight."

He managed a grin. "And to think I never believed you were listening to me, all those nights I tried to get you to eat your dinner," he said.

"I was listening," Heather said glibly. "I just wasn't hungry then."

"Well, I guess I'm just not hungry tonight. Sorry, honey. It's great ratatouille, though."

Heather was frowning at him. If he'd been in the frame of mind to be amused, he would have laughed at the reversal in their roles this week.

"I can't believe you're not hungry," she was saying. "You swam a whole mile before dinner."

"You were counting?"

Clint stood and cleared their plates away, scraping his uneaten dinner back into the big pot on the stove.

"No, but you always swim a mile when you're upset about something. Dad, why don't you just call her?"

Clint blinked. He'd barely had time to get used to the idea that he and Heather were becoming good friends, instead of constant antagonists. The notion of taking his daughter's advice on affairs of the heart was something he thought he might *never* get used to.

"Call who?" he said casually. "Laurie, you mean?"

"Give me a break." Heather's voice was long-suffering. "You've been upset ever since you came back from her place on Friday."

Clint busied himself with rinsing off the plates and stacking the dirty dishes in the dishwasher. Then he turned to Heather again, hoping the turbulence of his thoughts didn't show in his face.

"You're right," he said slowly. "The problem is that Laurie and I have some things to work out, and—well, we don't seem to be doing so well working them out, that's all."

"How are you going to get anywhere if you won't even call her?" Heather demanded, with perfect fifteen-year-old logic.

"It's not that simple, honey."

"Well, if you're sitting here waiting for her to call and she's sitting there waiting for you to call, I'm going to be pretty ticked off at both of you," was Heather's final pronouncement on the subject. "Listen, Janie said I could come over and watch a movie with her tonight. Is that okay? I'll be back by nine-thirty."

Absently Clint gave his permission. He was fleetingly aware of how much things had changed between Heather and him. Life was so much simpler now when she asked his permission, and he gave it willingly, sure that she'd be home when she said she would be. It was something he'd thought would never happen in the early dark days of her illness.

But even that thought didn't stay with him long. He watched her as she pulled on her hat and boots and then waved to her as she headed down the street to her friend Janie's house. Then he want right back to the problem he'd been worrying about all evening.

Should he call Laurie? Heather's refreshingly simple solution definitely had some appeal. He could just pick up the phone and say, "Listen, Laurie, we need to talk."

On the other hand, he'd been quite sincere when he'd told Heather that things weren't that simple. He'd been more badly hurt than he cared to admit when Laurie had turned down his request for help on Friday night.

Damn it, he'd tried everything to avoid asking her that favor! At first he'd been sure Heather would be fine on her own, but when she'd started to show symptoms of flu, he'd had second thoughts. His daughter still wasn't as strong as he would have liked her to be, and he knew a flu bug could escalate into big trouble if it wasn't watched carefully.

His first thought had been to call Dr. MacDonald, to see if he could help out. But the MacDonalds were away for the weekend, the answering service had informed him. Emergencies were being handled at the hospital.

Well, it was hardly an emergency, but Clint had started feeling uncharacteristically panicky then, as though he was sliding back into his old, isolated way of life after thinking he'd finally escaped from it. He didn't like the feeling.

After some hard thought, he'd approached the mother of one of Heather's closest friends, asking if Heather could stay there for the weekend. He hadn't been very surprised when the woman had politely turned him down, explaining that her three kids had just recovered from bad colds, and she wouldn't want either their germs or Heather's to make the rounds all over again.

He couldn't blame her for feeling that way. And he heard, under her reasonable excuse, a hint of reluctance to take on the responsibility for a diabetic teenager. He remembered his own initial fears on the subject. Hell, he was starting to feel them all over again.

That was when he'd turned to Laurie. He'd hated doing it, but surely she, of all people, would understand.

But she hadn't. She'd turned him down, cold. Well, not quite cold—he could still taste her lips against his whenever he thought about their encounter on her front porch. But even the wildflower sweetness of that kiss couldn't disguise what had really happened. He'd needed her and she'd let him down. The memory of it was like a knife in his gut.

He'd ended up making a lightning-fast trip to Montreal, staying just long enough to shake some hands and talk his potential business partners into meeting with him in Timmins on Monday. It had taken some powerful persuading—the developers felt, as Clint once had himself, that Timmins lay somewhat beyond the ends of the known world—but he'd done it.

He only remembered the process vaguely. Throughout the business meetings, his thoughts had been on Laurie and his own searing sense of betrayal.

That's what happens when you count on other people, an inner voice had been taunting him ever since. *You can't really trust anyone but yourself.*

And yet, as Heather had pointed out, that realization wasn't doing him any good. He wasn't eating well, wasn't sleeping much at all, wasn't even having any luck knocking himself out with hard work and more exercise than an Olympic athlete in training.

Sighing, Clint finally acknowledged that his fifteen-year-old daughter was right. He should call Laurie, and have this out. Before he could change his mind, he pushed himself away from the kitchen counter and headed for the phone.

He got her answering machine. Well, that wasn't so surprising. He left a brief message, and then wondered if she was working late at the office; he knew she sometimes added extra hours to accommodate her patients. When he got the machine there too, he hung up before the beep and headed back to his exercise room, intending to row and pedal and lift weights and generally work his system to its limits until Laurie called him back.

Laurie had forgotten to pack any shoes. In the midst of packing, she'd shoved her feet into her heavy winter boots, and the last thing on her mind as she'd left Timmins had been what she would wear when she got to Metro Toronto.

She arrived at the height of rush hour, and it seemed to take forever to get to her brother's apartment in the far reaches of Scarborough, one of Metro's suburban cities. The neighbor who'd agreed to watch the little girls overnight had stayed, waiting for Laurie, but the favor had made her late for work, and she hadn't been shy about saying so. Even Laurie's profuse thanks hadn't cheered the woman up, and Laurie was left with a bad taste before she'd even had time to take off her coat.

The mood her two little nieces were in didn't help any, either. Two-year-old Nicole had some vague idea who Laurie was, but of course one-year-old Lauren, her namesake, was too young to remember her aunt. Both were bewildered, understandably, and with the intuition of very young children, they had picked up on the fact that something was wrong in their lives. They had both been crying when Laurie arrived, and it took a long time to settle them down.

When they were finally sleeping, Laurie called the hospital to find out how Barry and Rhonda were doing. To her relief, she was actually able to talk to her brother. He'd escaped from the crash with fairly minor injuries: a broken shoulder, some bruised ribs and a mild concussion.

"I don't know why they won't let me go home," he said, "but to tell you the truth, I'm almost just as glad to stay here with Rhonda, except that I miss the girls."

"Doctors like to keep an eye on concussions," Laurie told him. "And if your ribs got banged up, you probably don't feel much like moving around, anyway."

"You can say that again." She could hear his grunt of pain as he moved in the hospital bed. "If I could donate my ribs to the guy who hit us, I'd do it happily."

As they spoke, Laurie felt the familiar mantle of responsibility slipping back into place around her shoulders. She was the reassuring one, the one in charge. She'd always been the family member the others turned to when they needed to lean on someone; even her father, before his death three years ago, had always called Laurie when he wanted advice about something.

She knew she was good in this role. It came naturally to her; she had a talent for helping people. But along with the familiar big-sister position there were a lot of other feelings swirling around in her brain. *I can't be everything to everybody,* she wanted to shout, while she calmly discussed bandaged ribs and broken legs with her younger brother. *Who is there for me to lean on?*

What made it worse was that she knew whom she wanted to lean on, but he wasn't there for her. He was nursing his old wounds up in Timmins, and she knew she was crazy to wish he could be here with her. She'd been catapulted into this chaotic household full of newly awakened, crying babies who needed to be changed, bathed, fed, and transported to the hospital on public transportation; ringing phones, long-distance consultations with friends and colleagues; and tired feet encased in three pairs of socks because in the midst of everything, she'd had no time to go out and buy herself a pair of shoes. Frankly, it wasn't a situation she could picture Clint Daniels volunteering to be part of.

By Friday morning, Laurie felt as though she'd been in the spin cycle of the automatic dryer for four days. And thank goodness for that dryer, she'd thought a dozen times, as she'd popped yet another load of baby laundry into the machine. The girls had been more than a handful, disturbed by the change in their routine and missing their parents. Every day Laurie had bundled them up and put them in their double stroller, managing somehow to get all three of them onto the bus to the subway, and then onto a streetcar that took them to the hospital's door. It did both parents and children a lot of good to have some time together, but the daily crosstown adventure was wearing Laurie out.

Her sister-in-law was suspended from the ceiling by a nest of ropes that looked like the rigging of an old-fashioned schooner, and Laurie soon realized from the extent of her injuries that Rhonda wouldn't be able to cope with the girls on her own any time soon.

"I feel like a hammock," Rhonda had complained laughingly on the second day.

Laurie had smiled in answer, and said something comforting about the speed at which Rhonda seemed to be mending. But inside, she was uneasy. Barry's job at a growing computer software firm was a demanding one, and the family needed his income. He'd have to get back to work as soon as he could, and how would Rhonda cope with the girls, when three of her limbs were encased in plaster?

For Laurie, the hardest time was when she was alone in the apartment at night, after the last load of laundry had been washed and dried and the kitchen cleaned up, the phone calls answered and a message left at the delivery service that if they didn't send over the groceries she'd ordered soon, there would be food riots in Apartment 1015. It was then that Laurie felt the full effect of the war inside her, between her strong sense of family and wanting to help out, and her need to get on with her own life. She wanted to be back with her patients, helping them in the carefully limited but caring way that she found so satisfying.

And she wanted... Well, she might as well admit it to herself, since there was no one here to listen or to see the tears that came to her eyes in spite of all her efforts to hold them back. She wanted Clint to help her, to take some of the burden when she felt this overwrought. She wanted his broad shoulders to lean against when she was tired like this. She wanted his strong hand to hold, and his sympathetic blue eyes to gaze into. She wanted him around, not just now, but always.

To face the fact that at this point, it didn't look like she was ever going to get any of those things, was harder than anything she'd ever done.

Clint was in a foul mood. He knew exactly what Heather was going to ask him when she walked in the door after school today, and he had his answer all ready for her.

Well, if she won't return my calls, what am I supposed to do? He'd done more than his share in trying to reach Laurie, he thought, as he poured himself a beer and headed down to the living room with it. Normally he didn't drink before dinner, but today he needed some help unwinding. He flicked on the lights in his big, empty main floor, and strode across to the sofa, knowing perfectly well that nothing was going to help him relax except getting things sorted out with Laurie.

Damn it, why hadn't she called him back? He'd left three messages, two brief and to the point, the third longer and half-joking, telling her he needed her professional services, because he didn't seem to be interested in food these days and he suspected it had something to do with being separated from her. He'd counted on getting an answer to that one, but so far, he hadn't.

He could just call her at work, he knew. But stubborn pride was making him hold out, telling him he'd done his part, and the rest was up to Laurie. Part of him was still hurt by her refusal of a week ago, and it wasn't something he could easily get over.

But all the stubborn pride in the world couldn't hold back the flood of memories that swept over him as soon as he'd settled himself onto the sofa. Clint closed his eyes, instantly carried back to that night he'd lain here with Laurie after Heather's frightening seizure. He could almost see the sleep-tangled dark mass of Laurie's hair, and smell the sweet, subtle perfume of her skin.

All the pent-up longing he'd felt that night came back to him, too, and he felt his stomach clench with an overpowering need to see Laurie. She'd taught him to be human again, after all those years of determined isolation. Maybe the weight of his demands on her had just been too heavy, or too sudden. Maybe they could start again, and move more slowly this time.

Maybe he should just swallow his pride and call her at work. Clint set down his untasted beer and reached for the phone. It was just five-thirty; he should be able to catch her.

"Laurie Houston's office." Clint recognized Nelson's young voice.

"Is Laurie still in?" he asked, trying to mask his own eagerness.

"I'm sorry, she's not. Is there any message?"

Clint was on the point of leaving yet another brief message for her to call him, when he changed his mind. "Can I reach her at home, do you know?"

"No. She's out of town."

Clint raised his eyebrows. Laurie hadn't mentioned any plans to go away. He asked Nelson when she would be back.

"I wish I could tell you. But she's been called away on a a family emergency, and she's not sure yet when she'll be home. It's Mr. Daniels, isn't it?"

Clint admitted absently that it was. His mind was racing, trying to imagine what Laurie must be feeling. He knew—better than most, at this point—how she felt about being the one who was called on to fix everyone else's problems.

"Well, Heather's next appointment isn't until next Thursday, and I'm pretty sure Laurie will be back by then. Why don't I give you a call if—"

Clint cut the boy off. "Actually, I wasn't thinking about Heather's appointment," he said. "Look, Nelson, I need to ask you a couple of favors."

This time, he got the favors he asked for. And this time, when Heather walked in the front door with questions about Laurie on her lips, Clint had a good answer all ready for her.

The weather was the final straw. Laurie actually found herself feeling nostalgic for the clean coldness of Timmins's endless winters, when she contrasted that with Toronto's messy, slushy early spring. It was March, and everything was soggy and gray, including the stuff coming down from the clouds.

"Go ahead, rain all over us," she muttered, as she maneuvered the double stroller out the front door for the daily visit to the hospital. "Or can't you make up your mind whether to rain or snow?"

"Rain or snow." Her older niece, Nicole, picked up the phrase, as she'd been doing all week with nearly everything Laurie said. The little girl made a singsong game out of new words. "Rain or snow, rain or snow," she repeated over and over.

Laurie grinned, but tiredly. "How about, wet miserable slush?" she said. "That's more to the point."

Nicole preferred "rain or snow," and she continued chanting it as they made their way down the front walk. The baby was in a peevish mood today, and she raised her voice, too, competing with her sister. Good Lord, Laurie thought, how do parents cope with these constant high-pitched little voices all day long?

She knew most of the problem was that she'd heard little else for the past five days. One afternoon she'd broken down and arranged to hire a baby-sitter for a couple of hours, just so she could go out and buy some groceries and a pair of shoes, but the woman had canceled on her at the last minute, and Laurie had spent the afternoon unsuccessfully trying to find a replacement.

When they reached the sidewalk, Laurie paused, trying to decide whether it was worth spending some extra money to take a cab to the subway today. She'd bundled the girls up as warmly as she could—a major feat of physical engineering, and one that had left her feeling exhausted before their trip had even started—but the idea of walking to the bus stop in this pelting slushy snow didn't appeal to her. She was just debating the alternatives, wondering if she really wanted to struggle with doors and locks again to get back into the apartment and call a cab, when a car pulled up directly in front of her.

Her first thought was that the people inside must want to ask directions, and she got ready to say that the only place she knew how to find was the bus stop down the street. Then she realized that the person who'd rolled down the passenger window was no stranger.

"Hi, Laurie." Heather Daniels looked delighted at the surprise on Laurie's face. "Nice day, isn't it? Can we give you a ride?"

It wasn't Clint's Volvo they were in. Laurie's mind took in one disconnected detail at a time. It must be a rental car, she thought. But most rental cars didn't come with baby seats—two of them—already buckled into the back seat.

She blinked. Heather was still smiling at her. A falling drop of slush landed on Laurie's nose, like a reminder that she was just standing there not saying anything.

She couldn't. She was too astonished. And when the door on the driver's side opened a moment later and Clint stepped out in his familiar sheepskin coat and a disgustingly smug grin, Laurie was even more at a loss for words.

"Where are you headed?" was all he said. Laurie wanted to demand the whole story, to find out how he'd materialized out of thin air. She wanted to tell him how she'd missed him, and how much time she'd spent thinking about him. She wanted to wrap her arms around him and never let him go.

Instead, she said, "We're on our way to the hospital. I was just trying to decide if I should call a cab."

"Well, you don't have to wonder anymore. Heather and I will ferry you to the hospital, assuming that contraption will fold up and fit into the trunk."

He seemed to have chosen the rental car with babies in mind. The trunk was huge, with more than enough room for the folded-up stroller. He and Heather hadn't brought much with them, Laurie noticed, just a couple of small overnight bags. And there, beside the two bags, was a suitcase she recognized. It was one of her own.

Seeing her glance at it, Clint explained, "We got Nelson to let us into your house. I thought you might appreciate a few more things to wear."

Laurie knew it was ridiculous to be thinking about her feet at a time like this. But she was so tired of padding around in all those layers of socks, feeling like Bigfoot.

"You didn't happen to bring any shoes, did you?" she asked.

"Sure. Slippers and running shoes. Is that all right?"

"Clint, you're a genius!"

She couldn't help it. She stood up on the tips of her heavy winter boots, and put her arms around him, hugging him as hard as she could. After a moment of startled hesitation, Clint hugged her back, and she felt the solid warmth of him like a welcome preview of summer. For the moment, the falling slush and her wet feet and the mammoth undertaking of transporting two small girls from Scarborough to the hospital simply didn't exist.

Then Heather's voice reached them from the back seat of the rental car. "When you guys are done," she said, with exaggerated teenaged patience, "the three of us are ready to go."

Once again, Clint had come into her world like a tornado. Before Laurie knew it, they were downtown, pulling up at the hospital's front door. It was heaven to sit back in the front seat and let Clint negotiate the city traffic.

"You must have been a cab driver in a previous life," she commented. "You seem to know every shortcut in town."

He grinned at her. "I'm just a speedy guy," he said, and then added, under his breath, "Well, most of the time, anyway." The gleam in his blue eyes was wicked and inviting, and Laurie caught her breath at the suggestiveness of it.

Heather, in the back seat, was busy unbuckling the girls, and had missed Clint's words. Laurie's heart had started to pick up speed, and when he laid a hand over hers, and she felt the pulsing heat from him, she had to admit, "You can't imagine how much I've been thinking of you, Clint."

He gave a brief snort. "Oh, I can imagine it, all right," he said. "Let's get that stroller out. Heather's way ahead of us."

Heather did seem to have a natural talent for dealing with babies, Laurie discovered. The girl insisted on taking charge of the stroller, wheeling it toward the elevator with practiced authority. Laurie had to laugh.

"Looks like Heather's talked herself into another job," she said, following with Clint.

"Do you mind?" He seemed to be watching her closely.

"Not in the least. I've been trying to be cook, nanny, housekeeper, receptionist, and nurse all week. I'm more than happy to hand some of the load over to someone else."

"Good." Clint paused as they reached the elevator. "I'll take over the 'cook' part, all right? I'm going to go and get some groceries while you're visiting here. What time should I pick you up?"

Laurie felt a powerful reluctance to let him leave her. He was like a lifeline, reminding her that she wasn't alone with all the responsibilities in the world. And more than that, she hated to see him go without having a chance to talk over everything that was on her mind. There were still so many unresolved questions between them.

On the other hand, the larder was pretty bare. She set a time, and squeezed his hand before stepping into the elevator. "You're saving the day, Mr. Daniels," she said softly.

"Happy to oblige, Ms. Houston."

And he *did* seem happy. That was what Laurie kept dwelling on while she was visiting her brother and sister-in-law. What had happened to the angry, taciturn man she'd last seen on her front porch on that bitter cold Friday night? Then, he'd seemed determined to cut himself off from everything they'd started to build together. But today he was acting as if nothing was more natural than for him to swoop down out of nowhere and take all her worries away.

And he'd brought her something to wear on her feet. Maybe she'd died and gone to heaven.

It was pretty close to heaven to have Heather there to play with her nieces, keeping an eye on them and lifting them up and down from floor to bed. For one thing, it gave Laurie a chance to do what she'd been meaning to do all week, which was to visit the office and straighten out the necessary paperwork for getting Barry and Rhonda transferred to a hospital closer to home as soon as possible. It took some arguing, but in the end Laurie was told that the specialist Rhonda needed to see would be able to treat her in Scarborough.

This minor victory raised her sister-in-law's spirits by a mile. "Laurie, that's great," Rhonda said. "That means when Barry goes home, I'll be close by."

On previous days in the week, it had taken Laurie an hour and a half to get home from the hospital. By then it had already been past dinnertime, and she'd had two fractious girls to deal with while she'd tried to get food on the table for all three of them.

But today, Clint magically transported them back to Barry and Rhonda's apartment with the same speed as their original trip to the hospital, and once again Heather took over the formerly difficult job of getting the girls out of their stroller and their winter clothes. Most miraculous of all, Clint took over in the kitchen, filling the empty refrigerator with the food he'd bought, and starting immediately to cook dinner.

"I can cook the babies' food," Laurie called to him, as she unpacked her suitcase and snuggled her feet into her slippers.

"Forget it." His reply was nearly lost amidst the clanging of pots and pans. "Were you feeding them on pizza last night?"

She smiled, picturing the pizza box she hadn't thrown out yet. "It was the night before last," she told him. "I haven't had a chance to clean up yet. And it was *me* I was feeding on pizza. Are you sure you know what to feed a one-year-old and a two-year-old?"

"Trust me. A man who can master a diabetic diet can conquer the world."

She was more than happy to trust him. For one thing, letting Clint cook gave her some time to make a few phone calls regarding a temporary housekeeper and baby-sitter to cover Barry. She simply hadn't had an uninterrupted half hour to make the arrangements before this.

By the time she'd satisfactorily lined someone up, through the local hospital's home-care program, Clint had dinner on the table. Laurie ate as though she hadn't seen food in a week, and Heather and Clint laughed at her.

"Better than pizza?" he'd teased.

"*Much* better. Heather, did you feed happy pills to those girls? They haven't been this smiley since I got here."

She knew perfectly well the girls were just responding to the lightened atmosphere, and that their peevishness all week had been an answer to Laurie's own frustration and loneliness. Which reminded her...

"Clint," she said, when dinner was over, "I haven't asked you—"

"It's all right," he said, holding up a hand. "Next week is school vacation, so Heather and I can stay as long as you need us."

Then he disappeared into the kitchen. She heard him whistling as he started washing the dishes.

"Heather," Laurie said, "your father is behaving very strangely."

"I know." Heather looked up from the floor, where she was constructing a tunnel of sofa cushions with Nicole. "Isn't it great?"

It *was* great, but it was also mystifying. Laurie spent the rest of the evening laundering sheets and towels, and helping Heather bathe the girls, so there wasn't a chance to talk to Clint privately. Once the babies were in bed, Heather's eyes were drooping, too, and Laurie made up the sofa for the girl to sleep on.

"I don't blame her for being tired," she said to Clint, as the two of them quietly finished cleaning up the kitchen. Heather had dropped instantly off to sleep in the darkened living room. "Keeping up with two little girls is enough to wear anybody out." Which reminded her...

"Want a hand making up the other bed?" He spoke before she could frame any of the questions she wanted to ask, and it wasn't until they faced each other over the big double bed that she found words for what she wanted to say. The clean sheets lay between them like a promise of passion to come, and they both knew it, but first there were things Laurie had to know.

"Clint, a week ago I had the feeling you wanted me out of your life," she said bluntly. "What happened to change your mind?"

And how far *have* you changed it? she wanted to add. Was this rescue a temporary favor, or something more?

He was frowning now, apparently concentrating on stuffing a fat pillow into its case. When he spoke, he was looking at the pillow, not at Laurie.

"I've known since the day I met you that there was no way I wanted you out of my life," he said slowly. "But it took me a long time to come to terms with what it really means to share a life with another person. I haven't had any experience at doing that," he added, smiling a little sheepishly. "There's never been anyone I wanted to share with, in that way."

"I had the feeling you were testing me out," she said, "trying to see how things would go."

He nodded seriously. "That's exactly what I was doing," he admitted. "I was spooked, Laurie. I didn't know what I was getting myself into. And last Friday night, when I wanted you to look after Heather for me—well, I guess that was another kind of test, to see how far I could trust you into my life."

"And I flunked the test." She didn't mince words.

"No. *I* flunked it, for reacting the way I did. I had no right to demand that you solve all my problems for me."

"I should have been readier to help you solve them," Laurie said carefully. "But I guess I've had a few demons of my own to get past, Clint. I've been wrestling with them all week, and feeling as though the weight of the whole world is on my shoulders. I've never been good at dealing with that feeling gracefully."

"I think you're right," he told her. "I think we both ran away from a sticky situation because we'd been hurt by the past."

"Then what changed things?" she asked. Her voice was soft, her eyes never moving from his. "Why did you follow me here?"

She loved the way that slow smile transformed his face, creasing the lines around his eyes. "Because having run away from the situation, all I could think of was how much I wanted to run right back again—how much I had to be with you, even though things might be difficult. When Nelson told me about your family's accident in the city, I realized right then that I *especially* wanted to be with you when things were difficult. And I knew then that I had to come, to prove to you that I wouldn't ask you to share my problems again without being willing to share yours, too."

Laurie felt an unexpected trembling in her limbs, as though she were becoming weightless. The way Clint was smiling at her across the newly made bed was so seductive she could barely force her mind to work through what he'd just said. But she knew that the trembling was from far more than thoughts of making love with him. It was his admission of just how much he wanted to share with her that was making her heart beat with such giddy joy.

"Clint," she said, caught between laughter and sudden tears, "I knew we could find an answer to this."

"Oh, that's not the answer."

His words were deliberately offhand, but Laurie could see that his heart, too, was beating faster. The hollow at the base of his neck betrayed his quickening pulse.

"It's not?" She blinked at him.

"No. That just spells out the question. The answer is this."

With a casualness that didn't fool her at all, he reached into his pocket and pulled out a small box. She felt her eyes widen, as every half-hidden hope she'd nursed about this maddening, powerful, lovable man came shooting to the surface.

"I love you, Laurie." The words made her feel as though a summer breeze had just wafted through the room. "And I don't ever want to have to spend another week leaving messages on your damn answering machine and wondering if I'm going to see you again. So I'm proposing to you—that's my answer to the question. Will you marry me?"

Laurie knew her answer was in her face, and in her eyes, long before she let out a long breath and with it the words, "Oh, Clint, yes. Of course I'll marry you."

"And have babies with me?" He seemed determined to spell everything out.

"Yes to that, too. As long as I don't have to wrestle them in and out of strollers all by myself."

"You'll never have to do things all by yourself again," he assured her.

"And neither will you," she replied gently. "And that's the real answer, isn't it?"

She was never quite sure how they got from opposite sides of the bed to an intimate embrace in the middle of it. Some kind of athletic dive must have been required, she thought hazily, but she hadn't been aware of them having made it. All that mattered was being in the circle of Clint's arms, tasting his kisses, renewing their mutual passion now that they'd taken this final step toward a new life together.

Clint felt ridiculously light-headed. The sweet perfume of Laurie's skin acted on him like champagne. She wore her hair in a tousled ponytail; he reached up a hand and pulled it free, loving the way the thick strands surrounded his fingers.

"There's still one question we *haven't* answered," he told her. His words were lazy, competing for attention with the long curves of Laurie's body and the way his hands felt following them.

"What question is that?"

"Whatever happened to King Midas?"

She paused, then laughed. "I'd forgotten all about the poor man," she said.

"Well, I hadn't. It was really bugging me. You know, did the guy ever eat again, and what happened to his daughter?" He remembered his anger when she'd compared him to the king who'd turned his daughter into cold metal, and knew that he'd been angry because he'd known she was right.

"Did you ever look it up?"

"Yes. There was a library next to the grocery store where I went shopping today. I ran in and grabbed a book about Greek myths."

Laurie was practically purring under his loving hands, moving eagerly to meet his increasingly erotic caresses. "Well, you'd better tell me about it fast, because I'm rapidly losing interest."

"So am I. But here's the end of the story. It seems the same god who'd given Midas the golden gift in the first place came back through town again. And Midas asked if he could go back to being normal, please."

"I see." Laurie's voice was breathless, distracted by the way Clint's fingers were stroking her spine under the warm flannel of her shirt.

"So the god said all right, he'd take away the golden touch, but first Midas had to go and cleanse himself in the river."

"Lucky thing there was one handy."

"Oh, I suspect Midas had put one in for his private use. He was quite a swimmer, you know."

"You're making that up."

"*I'm* telling this story," he said in a mock-stern voice.

"Too bad there's no river handy." She was opening the buttons of his shirt as she spoke, running her fingers through the hair on his chest. "Think we could make do with the bathtub?"

"Sure. But not for a while yet. First I figured we'd get into some things that don't appear in the Midas story, if that's okay with you."

Laurie already felt as if she were floating, buoyed up by the incredible things Clint was making her feel. "That story was probably edited for family use, anyway," she said. Her sentence ended on a gasp, as he ran a possessive hand over the tight centers of her breasts.

"I guess we should get used to the idea of editing a lot of things for family use." His face told her how eagerly he was looking forward to the idea. "But not just now, all right?"

Their mouths merged hungrily, and as Laurie closed her eyes to the blissful humming inside her, she felt as though the single lamp at the head of the bed was shimmering and glowing, and turning the whole world to gold.

* * * * *

COMING NEXT MONTH

#667 WILD ABOUT HARRY—Linda Lael Miller
Widowed mom Amy Ryan was sure she wasn't ready to love again.
But why was she simply wild about Australia's *Man of the World,*
Harry Griffith?

#668 A FINE MADNESS—Kathleen Korbel
It seemed someone thought that England's *Man of the World,*
Matthew Spears, and Quinn Rutledge belonged together! Could they
survive an eccentric ghost's matchmaking antics and discover
romance on their own?

#669 ON HIS HONOR—Lucy Gordon
When Italy's *Man of the World,* Carlo Valetti, walked back into
Serena Fletcher's life, she was nervous. Was this sexy charmer there
to claim *her* love—or *his* daughter?

#670 LION OF THE DESERT—Barbara Faith
Morocco's *Man of the World,* Sheik Kadim al-Raji, had a mission—
to rescue Diane St. James from kidnappers. But once they were safe,
would this primitive male be able to let her go?

#671 FALCONER—Jennifer Greene
Shy Leigh Merrick knew life was no fairy tale, but then she met
Austria's *Man of the World,* roguish Rand Krieger. This lord of the
castle sent her heart soaring....

#672 SLADE'S WOMAN—BJ James
Fragile Beth Warren never dreamed she'd ever meet anyone like
America's *Man of the World,* Hunter Slade. But this solitary man just
wanted to be left alone....

AVAILABLE NOW:

Bestselling author NORA ROBERTS captures all the
romance, adventure, passion and excitement of Silhouette in
a special miniseries.

THE
CALHOUN WOMEN

Four charming, beautiful and fiercely independent
sisters set out on a search for a missing family
heirloom—an emerald necklace—and each finds
something even more precious... passionate romance.

Look for THE CALHOUN WOMEN miniseries
starting in June.

COURTING CATHERINE
in Silhouette Romance #801 (June/$2.50)

A MAN FOR AMANDA
in Silhouette Desire #649 (July/$2.75)

FOR THE LOVE OF LILAH
in Silhouette Special Edition #685 (August/$3.25)

SUZANNA'S SURRENDER
in Silhouette Intimate Moments #397 (September/$3.29)

 *Silhouette Books*